FOREVER FAMILY

DEANNA ROY

casey shay press

Forever Family

Casey Shay Press
PO Box 160116
Austin, TX 78716
www.caseyshaypress.com

Paperback: ISBN: 9781938150517

Ebook-ISBN: 9781938150524

Library of Congress: Control Number 2016932204

Other books by Deanna Roy

Forever Innocent
Part 1 of the Forever Series

Forever Loved
The shattering sequel to Forever Innocent

Forever Sheltered
Tina's story with Dr. Darion

Forever Bound
Jenny's story with songwriter Chance

Stella & Dane
A bad boy romance

Baby Dust: A Novel about Miscarriage
Women's fiction on baby loss

Jinnie Wishmaker
Marcus Mender
an adventure series for 9-12 year olds under the name DD Roy

Dust Bunnies: Secret Agents
an iPad story book app for children ages 3-9

Learn more about the author at
www.deannaroy.com

For my fans
My happily ever after
is with you

Go see all your dedications at the end!

1

CORABELLE

My father used to have a T-shirt that read "If it's too loud, you're too old."

Maybe I was getting too old.

I stood at the very front of an outrageous screaming crowd in a concert arena that I would swear held the entire student body of UC San Diego.

Next to me was Jenny, huge pregnant belly and all. I winced every time she jumped up and down, sure she was going to bounce the baby right out. Her happy voice squealed like a teenager. She kept bumping up against the chest-high metal wall that separated us from the stage.

The noise made my ears ring. Girls screaming. Guys shouting. The occasional screech of a lead guitar set to the wrong level.

Nobody was actually playing a song yet. The new wave of excitement came from some hunky guy in black who was testing a guitar. He had it cradled against his thigh, one shoulder thrown back, his fingers picking out an unbelievably fast set of notes that everyone else seemed to recognize. Or maybe they'd just scream for anything. The concert was already a half hour late. The crowd just wanted something to happen and encouraged anything that made it seem like the show was starting.

The lights blacked out onstage and a million colored beams rolled from the ceiling to the floor. It was just a test, but the cheers crescendoed one more time.

I tried to feel the magic of being amid all this energy. But it was so — pushy. Literally. I was getting shoved and manhandled from every direction. I wished Gavin were with us. I could have used the strong, broad protection of his body from the crush of the crowd. I didn't know how Jenny was doing it. When I was as pregnant as her, I barely ever left the sofa.

Except…I'd never been as pregnant as her. She'd passed the mark when I'd gone into early labor with Finn two weeks ago.

I squashed those thoughts immediately. I was not going to let my past intrude on this crazy night. Her husband-to-be, Chance, would be playing an opening number, not directly for megastar Dylan Wolf, not yet, but for the band that would open for Dylan. Chance was not on the fast track, for sure, but he had a record in production that everyone was pinning their hopes on.

Jenny didn't mind either way. Her face glowed happy in the blue light, waiting for Chance to come on. This was his last performance before their wedding next weekend. Then the baby would come in a few weeks.

I refused to harbor any jealousy over her happiness. It took willpower and control to keep my thoughts positive and happy, but I had managed so far, even when Jenny raced into my apartment with her DVD sonogram to show me the heartbeat. These were all moments I also remembered fondly. The real test would be when she brought her baby home.

I never got to do that.

The hunk with the guitar set it carefully in a stand and strode offstage. The crowd settled again. A few attempts to shout "Dylan, Dylan, Dylan!" started, then died out.

I glanced around. The floor of the arena was packed with the hard-core fans who had close-up tickets, and the first tier was pretty full. Up top, though, fans who didn't care about the opening singer were still filtering in.

I checked my watch. So behind schedule.

"Are they always late?" I asked Jenny.

She shrugged. "They watch how many are still coming in the gates."

We'd hung out backstage with Chance and the Sonic Kings until a security guard came for us. Since Chance played first, we had to be out there before the concert began. When Dylan came on later, his wife, Jessie, would join us in the front row.

The crowd was our first indication that something was about to happen. The roar surged again. They must see something we couldn't, up so close.

Then I caught movement at the back of the stage. Jenny clutched my hand as Chance came out. The response was tremendous, then faltered a little as the crowd realized it wasn't Dylan. But Chance was old hat at this by now, and started with a quip in his best southern drawl. "Y'all are waiting on the Dixie Chicks, right? Cuz I put on a bra for this."

The crowd laughed and settled in. He didn't introduce himself, not yet, but jumped right into the opening licks of one of his rock songs. On his own, he tended to stay a little closer to the country end of the spectrum, but he knew what Dylan's fans were looking for.

I held on to Jenny as she jumped in place. I tried not to picture the baby sloshing in there. Her ankles and wrists were something to behold, swollen to the point that she could only wear flip-flops, and her six-inch tangle of bracelets was a thing of the past.

Luckily, San Diego didn't get all that cold, even in November. So she was getting away with her summer footwear. Although she might lose a shoe if she kept jumping like she was.

Chance looked our direction and beamed. The song wasn't romantic, just a rock anthem about partying on a Saturday night, but Jenny was feeling it. I was happy for her. I really was.

I squeezed her hand and moved along with her. "He's so great!" I shouted in her ear.

She nodded at me. "I know!"

The lights shifted and turned as Chance moved across the stage. He didn't get the big treatment like Dylan would later, but it was a nice set. I moved with the music and let the party atmosphere take me away from my piles of work back home. Papers to grade as a lowly first-year teaching assistant at UCSD. My own courses to study for. A thesis to think about. I was just glad to have my bachelor's degree behind me. Life was moving forward. Most of it.

Chance finished out strong and the crowd roared. They had been won over. I knew Jenny always held her breath at this moment, worried they would start chanting for Dylan instead.

He didn't pause but went straight into the next number. Jenny relaxed and pressed her hand to her chest. "I think I might have jiggled my pee out," she said with a frown. "No more jumping."

"Good idea," I said.

She moved her hand to her belly. "He's kicking up a storm, though. The baby always gets riled at concerts."

My willpower faltered, and I swallowed the envy that threatened to rise up. I'd been lucky these past few years to avoid pregnant people. College was generally good like that. But here it was, right beside me, about to pop right out. I drew in a deep breath and focused on the music.

My life was happy. I had Manuelito, Gavin's five-year-old son, and he was good for me, just the most amazing kid. He was spending an extended holiday in Mexico with his mother. She would have him for Thanksgiving and Christmas and wouldn't be back until after the first of the year.

And Gavin would be graduating soon. We'd be able to build some savings soon, and maybe, just maybe, we could get his vasectomy reversed.

I couldn't act like my life hadn't gotten started. It wasn't true.

I was at a concert with my best friend, who was about to marry the hunky singer onstage.

I had the love of my life back and a sweet little family.

I had graduated — finally — and made my goal of becoming a TA in graduate school.

Everything was fine. I would not be shaken.

I would live each moment as it came. I'd keep believing that the thing I wanted most of all, a baby of my own, would happen eventually. I would have faith.

2

JENNY

I swear I could feel each drumbeat in my belly.

The sound crashed over me, thumping through my waterlogged middle like a rock-and-roll sonogram.

I swayed with it, hoping I was keeping the baby chilled out despite the noise. Sometimes the little bub would startle at a loud noise, making a swift little lurch.

I kept my hands on the metal gate that held us back several feet from the stage. This was the first time I'd encountered it. But after a few girls had climbed up and gotten way too frisky with Dylan at a concert in Atlanta, the security guards decided to limit direct access to the stage floor.

I didn't like it. The wall caused a couple of problems for me. One, it bummed me out because this was the last concert I'd be able to attend for Chance before the baby came. And I couldn't get up to him. He often reached down and took my hand during our favorite song, and this time, he couldn't.

But also, these creepy girls were pushing against me. Hard. As they jostled, I had to hold on to the gate and keep my arms strong so that I wouldn't crush my belly.

Another overly energetic woman fell into me, and I snapped. "Watch where you're gyrating!" I yelled. "Baby." I pointed to my belly.

She rolled her eyes. "You shouldn't even be here."

That was it. I'd had it. I turned in to her and shoved my elbow straight into her gut. Corabelle grabbed my arm. "Jenny!"

"You're crazy!" the girl said, but had the sense to head away from us.

Corabelle kept her grip on me. "You all right?" she asked. Her eyes darted nervously up to the stage.

Chance was on the other end, making his way back, singing his heart out. And I was missing it. "I'm fine," I said, and lifted my chin.

The song rollicked along. My anger drained out of me, and suddenly I was super exhausted. I clutched at the gate. Maybe we should have stayed in the stage wings instead of coming out on the floor. I'd have been more comfortable.

But it just wasn't the same back there. For his last concert, I wanted to be out here.

I took deep breaths and steeled myself to make it through. We wouldn't stay for the other bands, not even Dylan. Just hang out in the dressing rooms with Chance and listen to the concert piped in. There was always a buffet and lots of fun talk. I could put my feet up and soak up the last of the fun life before the baby came.

It was a great life, and I enjoyed it.

The drummer blasted the final three cymbal strikes for the end of the song, and Chance took a moment to introduce himself and the band. He picked at his guitar, strumming a few single notes that I recognized. Yes, he was going to slow it down now. I let out a long exhale in relief. He was going to play our special one.

"I wrote this little ditty a few months ago," he said, "when that lovely lady agreed to be my wife." He pointed at me and the crowd turned.

I saw with great satisfaction that the rude girl noticed and frowned. Ha.

"So, this here is an original of mine, called 'Forever.'"

The opening chords flooded me with calmness. I held on tight to the top of the wall as Chance's rich voice filled the arena.

There ain't nothing you can say
To make me turn away
There ain't nothing you can do
To ever take my love away from you
Because I said forever
And that's just what I'm gonna do

I tried to always listen to the song like it was the first time I heard it. I wanted always to believe it. Corabelle squeezed my arm. She got it. She had found her forever too.

I swayed along with the music. The crowd didn't know the words. It had never been released. Maybe it would someday, if Chance got a break. Right now, he could sing to a crowd like this, but if they searched for him later, they couldn't get his work.

Soon. Hopefully. If this record deal worked out.

I wanted to revel in the music. It was so different in a huge arena than in a small bar or private party, where Chance played most of the time.

But my bladder wasn't cooperating.

The pressure was low and heavy. I knew it well. I wouldn't be able to hold it long, and now I was in the danger zone. If I sneezed or coughed or even laughed too hard, it would leak.

God, the stuff about pregnancy nobody told you.

Chance looked my direction, like he was singing to me. I knew he couldn't see me easily, as the stage lights were blinding as you looked out. But he always knew where I was.

I tried to feel it, really let it sink in.

But my bladder. The pressure.

I felt a tickle in my throat from all the cheering. No no no. I was going to cough.

The urge was strong, but I clamped it down. I tried to gather spit so I could swallow and make my throat calm. It seemed to work. I thought I had it under control. Then it just burst out. My insides clamped down, and I coughed.

Crap. The pee was going to let go.

I felt the water come out. Then run down my legs. And keep coming.

Shit. Really? All of it? That bad?

My face flooded crimson. I was wearing a long skirt, thank God, so nobody could really see. But it was running down to my ankles and making my shoes squishy.

So gross.

I smiled at Chance and thought — let me get through this song and we'll go. Forget the concert, the after-party. Just get home and get cleaned up.

Chance belted out the chorus, but I could barely hear him for the roar in my ears. Something was different. Wrong. I let go of the gate and clutched my belly.

I felt emptier. I couldn't explain it. But I was less taut or something. Less full.

Then it hit.

The contraction rippled across my body like someone had wrung out a cloth. I felt squeezed. I forgot all about the concert and turned to Corabelle. "Something's wrong," I said, but my voice barely worked. It was like I didn't have any breath.

"What?" Corabelle asked, leaning in. But then she turned to look at me and saw my face. "Oh my God," she said. "Let's go."

I glanced back up at Chance. I knew he couldn't make us out clearly, not with the lights. He wouldn't see my expression or my fear. I waved at him. He could see the movement and nodded with a smile.

But I was panicked.

Corabelle pulled me through the crowd. I kept my eyes on Chance. He probably thought I had to pee. I had no way to tell him.

We made it through the throng to the backstage security guard to the left of the stage. By the time we got there, I was feeling worse, sick, and in pain.

"We need help," Corabelle said. "Is there an ambulance here?"

"NO!" I told her. "Not without Chance!" But just that much talking made something happen, another strong cramp gripping me tight. I doubled over. Even without my trying, my body started a huffing sort of breath.

One of the stage managers, a broad teddy-bear-sized man named Todd, came up to wrap his arm around me. "You okay?"

I tried to get words out. "I…think…my…water broke."

"What?" Corabelle exclaimed. "When?"

"During…the song." The contraction slowed down and I gasped for breath.

She looked down at my feet. "Get the EMTs," she told Todd. "She's not due for another five weeks."

This made Todd move. He dashed over to the security guard and yanked a radio from his belt. He mashed a button and shouted into it. I didn't pay a lot of attention, staring at the floor, trying to bring down my panic.

Corabelle gripped me, holding me up. "Can you walk?" she asked.

"In a second," I managed to say. It was easing up. After a couple more breaths, I was able to stand up straight again. "Maybe it's just those Braxton Hicks or whatever?"

Corabelle shook her head. "Not if your water broke."

She was right. "Is it too soon?" I thought of Corabelle's baby, born so early. He hadn't made it, and died on his seventh day. Panic flooded me.

"You're fine," she said. "Finn had a heart condition, remember? That's why he died, not being premature."

But her eyes didn't match her words. She was scared.

"Come this way," Todd said, leading us away from the stage. He still held on to the guard's radio. We took small steps toward the back hallway, where the dressing rooms were. I wasn't sure what I wanted more, a sofa or an ambulance.

The guard followed us. "They always have EMTs at the arena for things like this," he said. "They are coming down."

But suddenly I felt fine, like really fine. I straightened my back, checked for cramps, pain, weirdness.

Nothing. The baby elbowed my belly as if to say, "Get over it."

Now I was embarrassed.

"I think I'm okay," I said. "Maybe it was something else?"

Todd stopped in his tracks. "Is this one of those false alarms? My brother's wife dragged him to the hospital three times before she finally popped out my nephew."

"Why don't you go to the bathroom and check things?" Corabelle said. "Be sure."

I nodded as Todd opened the door to Chance's dressing room. It was small and empty, the holding area for the low men on the concert totem pole.

But it had a bathroom. I headed for it, pushing inside. I felt silly. Maybe I really had just peed myself.

I went inside and stared at myself in the mirror below the hot overhead lights, my face pale and washed out. The dull brown of my natural hair color showed through the pink chalk I'd been applying to cover the roots, since I couldn't dye my hair anymore.

My mascara-heavy lashes were garish and sad. I'd bitten off my lipstick, leaving the plum liner standing out around the edges, like a coloring-book mouth nobody had bothered to fill in.

I looked like a tabloid train wreck.

And I'd peed myself.

I turned on the water and wet a paper towel, fixing the smudges of black beneath my eyes. Then I wet some more to take with me into the bathroom for the cleanup.

Maybe I would have to wear adult diapers.

I could borrow from the baby.

Tears sprang in my eyes at the thought. Nobody said pregnancy would be like this. Out in the arena, scantily clad girls were clamoring for Chance's attention.

And I was a pee-soaked, bad-haired, pale-faced washout.

The toilet was inside a little stall even though it was the only one. I pushed the door inside and turned around to lift the long skirt. This was so awful. The lowest of lows.

I had just reached for my panties, soaked in all the wrong ways, when the next contraction hit. I cried out, gripping the sides of the stall.

The fullness hit me again, and I realized — that's the baby.

The baby was coming.

"Corabelle!" I screamed.

She came instantly, crashing through the door. "Jenny?"

"Where are the EMTs?" My voice was starting to go, lost in the huffy breathing.

"They're out here. Waiting for you." She took my hand. "Can you walk at all?"

I forced my foot to take a step forward. It obeyed. I clutched at Corabelle, hanging on to her arm like a lifeline. We made a few more mincing steps toward the door.

"You're seven minutes apart," she said. "That's not too bad. You'll make it."

I nodded, glad somebody knew what they were doing. We made it to the door and passed back into the main room. A man and a woman in navy uniforms were waiting, already wearing latex gloves. Behind them was a rolling stretcher. It looked like heaven.

I fixated on their hands in the beige rubber, imagining my baby getting caught by them. This calmed me, knowing they were prepped and ready. I had a place to lie down. They would take me where I needed to go. It would be okay.

I felt remarkably calm.

"How far along are you?" the man asked.

"She's thirty-five weeks," Corabelle said. "Her water broke."

The man turned to me. "Let's get you up on the stretcher," he said. "We're going to need to transport you."

Suddenly my calm snapped. "No!" I shouted. "Not without Chance!"

"A chance for what?" the woman asked. She had come around to my other side and the two of them were leading me to the stretcher.

I planted my feet. "My fiancé! I want him!"

"Where is he?" the man asked.

Todd stepped forward. "He's onstage. I've already ordered the crew to end his show."

The contraction started to ease and I bent over, bracing my hands on my knees. "Thank you," I told Todd. "Thank you so much."

He patted my back. "You're going to be fine."

But Corabelle was in a fury. "Do you not realize the situation we're in? This baby is NOT DUE. We have a PREMATURE INFANT. Get up there!" She pushed me toward the stretcher.

I dug in. I'd never seen her face so red, but I was not about to leave without Chance. "Back off, Cora," I said. "Chance is coming with me."

"Let's get you ready to go," the male EMT said. "We won't leave until you say so."

I didn't trust any of them. I backed away, shaking my arms to get myself loose. "I'm not going anywhere. You can't make me. I can refuse transport. I know how this works."

"Ma'am, you do not want to have a baby in a concert arena," the male EMT said. "Let's get you up. We'll collect your husband."

Oh my God. He wasn't my husband. Not yet.

"We have to get married!" I said. "Now!"

"You're in labor!" Corabelle said. "There's no time for that!"

The contraction was long gone, so I flailed like Kermit the Frog. "Like hell this baby is coming before I have a marriage certificate!"

Corabelle's face was bright red now. "I really think you need to focus on the baby."

"I really think you need to back off!" I was being mean and confrontational, but God, the pain. Even with the contraction gone, my back was killing me. My whole body was revolting against the onslaught of unfamiliar muscle clenching.

Todd whipped around to us, the radio to his cheek. "Chance is on his way. They cut the set short."

"Will you get on the stretcher now?" Corabelle asked.

I didn't think I had a choice. The pain rolled through me like a tsunami, taking all my strength with it. I listed forward and the two EMTs caught me in their expert arms, lifting me up and onto the gurney.

Lying down was bliss, pure bliss. With no contraction, and no need to stand, everything collapsed inward. I actually fought sleep for a second, like I was passing out.

The EMT strapped a blood pressure cuff to my arm. I stared at the white rectangles on the ceiling. I realized for the first time that the concert noise had stopped and piped-in music had taken over. Chance would be here any second.

As if on cue, the door slammed open, smashing against the wall. "Jenny!" Chance shouted, careening across the room to lunge against the stretcher. "What happened?"

"I think I got a little too excited," I said.

"She's in labor," Corabelle said. "Seven minutes apart."

His beautiful eyebrows shot up. I stared at him like he was a mirage. Everything seemed fuzzy on the edges.

"Blood pressure is 180 over 115," the male EMT said. "That's high. Let's get her out the door."

The stretcher began to roll. I kept my gaze on Chance, jogging alongside us. An earbud was still clipped to his back collar. I reached for it, but my arm was rubbery. I was so tired. I bumped along as they wheeled me down the empty backstage hallway.

But the minute we pushed out the back door and into the cool evening air, I was revived. All the color flooded back and the hard edges returned and I realized — I'M HAVING A BABY AND NOT A WEDDING.

I tried to sit up and realized I was strapped to the gurney. "Stop!" I shouted. "I'm not having this baby today!"

"Darling, I don't think you have a say in the matter," Chance said.

We continued rolling toward the boxy yellow and blue EMT vehicle.

"No!" I said again, trying to find the buckles that held the straps in place. "I'm getting married first!"

"Jenny," Chance said, taking my hand to stop me from unlatching myself. "We didn't exactly do things the old-fashioned way. We'll have the wedding."

"Nooo," I said, imploring him with my eyes. "I know what happens in there. They'll put my last name on the baby's crib. For our whole lives, those pictures and documents will show that he was a Gillespie first and a McKenzie second."

I didn't cry much, but tears definitely spilled out of my eyes then. I meant it. I should never have waited so late to have the ceremony, but Chance and I had barely met when I got pregnant. We weren't sure about the marriage part until a couple months ago. I'd done things as fast as I could.

"Can you call the JP we hired?" I asked Chance. "See if he can come now?" We'd arrived at the ambulance and the EMTs were opening the doors.

Chance's face was genuinely pained. "Jenny, he's doing that other wedding tonight. Remember? He told us about it."

More tears spilled out. "Then I'm not going anywhere," I said stubbornly. "I'm not getting in the ambulance until we have somebody to marry us."

Todd caught up with us, still holding the stolen security radio. "Dylan's ordained. Remember how he married that Kardashian?"

I grabbed Chance's collar. "Get Dylan. NOW. We already have our license. We just need someone to do it."

Todd and Chance looked at each other.

"What are you waiting for?!" I didn't intend to end the sentence with a scream, but another contraction hit me mid-sentence, and I howled like a strangled cat. The EMTs froze in place.

Todd almost dropped the radio, but he buzzed through. Chance took my hand and tried to lead me through the breathing exercises we'd done in our birth preparation course. I elbowed him in the chest. "Stop it," I wheezed. "Just stop it!"

His face registered panic as he looked up at Corabelle. She shrugged. "It's not like the classes," she said.

I kept Chance's hand in a death grip. I knew this sucker would end eventually. Then we could get Dylan down here and do the words. He could sign the paper later. It would work. By the time it mattered what was filed where, we'd have it all squared away.

I turned back to Corabelle. "Call my mother. She'll get there when she can."

"Shall we put you inside now, ma'am?" the male EMT asked.

"No!" I said. "Not…until…we have…Dylan!"

The lights over the back parking lot had a haze over them. The pain was intense but the cool air helped. Maybe I'd just have the baby out here.

But he was early. Or she was. God, I would find out what we were having!

"Dylan's coming," Todd said. "The Titanium Overlords are going to extend their set to cover for him."

"NOW can we put you inside?" the female EMT asked.

I nodded, trying to breathe, trying to listen, and trying to stay in control of the situation.

This might be my finest hour.

The contraction began to settle as the EMTs slid the gurney into the back of the ambulance. Corabelle stayed down, her eyes wide, and I knew she was thinking about when she last rode in one, after almost drowning in the Pacific. Gavin had pulled her from the waves. What a day that had been.

Chance got in beside me.

"Come on," I said to Corabelle. "I need my witness!"

She climbed inside.

We heard footsteps approaching, then Dylan's face appeared in the door. "Hot damn," he said. "I always wanted to be part of an emergency wedding during the birth of a baby!"

"Get your ass in here," Chance said. "Jenny won't go to the hospital unless we're married."

Dylan hopped inside, glammed up for his concert. Behind him, a roadie with a video camera squeezed in.

"This is too many people for the capacity of this vehicle," the female EMT said sternly.

I tried to sit up again. "Then I'm not going."

"I'll get out," Corabelle said.

"No!" I glared at the EMT. "Kick yourself out if someone needs to go."

Chance waved to the male EMT, who was still standing outside. "Just go," he said. "It's only a few miles."

The female EMT tried to push forward, but the video camera guy aimed his lens at her. "Smile, you're about to be the most hated figure in a viral video!"

She hesitated. "I don't get paid enough for this," she said.

"We'll make sure you get a hefty Christmas check," Dylan said. He winked at the male EMT, who still waited on the ground outside the door.

"We good?" the EMT asked. He didn't wait for an answer, but shut the door.

"How are you going to get back?" Chance asked.

"Todd's following in his car," Dylan said. "We got it all taken care of." He grinned down at me like I was the best thing ever.

"Can we get more lights in this place?" the video guy asked.

The female EMT glared at him, and he shrank back. "I'm all good," he said.

Despite the ongoing pain, I felt elated. We were going to get this done. I wrapped both my hands around Chance's.

"You know what the hell you're doing?" Chance asked Dylan.

"It ain't rocket science," Dylan replied.

The video guy shifted toward Dylan and turned on a long, narrow light over the lens. "And…go," he said.

Dylan's face got all serious. "Mawwaige," he said. "Mawwaige is what bwings us together today."

Corabelle groaned, but I laughed. If we had to get married in an ambulance, between contractions, by a rock star who'd only been ordained so he could hook up a Kardashian, we might as well have a good time with it.

3

TINA

When I got the text from Corabelle that Jenny was getting married in an ambulance by the singer Dylan Wolf, I dropped my phone.

Darion looked up from his sketch pad. "Everything okay?"

"We have to go!" I told him.

I stuck the caps on all the open tubes of paint and rubbed my messy hands on my shirt. New stripes of color layered over all the splotches and spatters from other days.

Darion set down his charcoal. "What's going on?"

I lunged for my tennis shoes. "Jenny is in labor and getting married in an ambulance. If we can get to the intersection of Balboa and Clairemont in five minutes, we might catch them."

Darion stood up and tossed me a towel. I wiped my hands hastily and dug through the bowl by the door for my set of keys.

We raced down the hall, not bothering with the elevator. We took the stairs two and three at a time to get to the garage.

"Was that the spare car keys you grabbed?" he asked as we darted between cars, looking for his black Mercedes.

"Of course! No way was I going to wait on the valet!" Dang fancy condo and its snaillike doormen.

We spotted the car and dashed for it. Only when Darion was behind the wheel and heading out the exit did he ask, "Is the baby okay?"

"Corabelle didn't say. But she isn't due for over a month."

"That's premature, but not enough to cause serious issues, as long as the baby is healthy," Darion said. "Why the wedding?"

"Beats me. They only decided to get married a couple months ago."

We sped down a back street. The night was quiet in our residential neighborhood, but traffic picked up as soon as we headed into the Saturday evening nightlife.

Another text came through from Corabelle. I read it and told Darion, "They already passed through the light at Genesee. We should see them any minute."

"They're going to St. Anthony's, then?" Darion asked. "We could meet them there."

"She wants me to be a witness and they'll be married before we get there," I said. I peered out the window as we approached the intersection.

"Are they in lights and siren?" Darion asked.

"I see lights!" I said, pointing.

"Got it," Darion said. He careened across two lanes to swing into the small parking lot of a gas station.

We leaped from the car and took off down the middle of the street toward the whirl of lights. The vehicle didn't seem to be slowing down.

"You sure this is the right ambulance?" Darion yelled as we approached.

"We're going to look pretty crazy if it isn't!" I said.

The ambulance passed us, lights flashing, but no sirens. We stopped in the middle of the street, watching it go by. "They're not supposed to stop," Darion said. "They could get in a lot of trouble if they do."

But even as he said it, the brake lights lit up. When it came to a stop, the back door popped open and none other than Dylan Wolf appeared. "Come on in, the party's just getting started!"

I rushed up to the bumper and took Dylan's hand to get a leg up. I immediately bumped against the back of the stretcher where Jenny was strapped in. She was panting, her hair leaving pink chalk on the white pillow.

"We're having a contraction break in the ceremony," Dylan said.

"You can't let anyone else in here!" a woman in an EMT uniform protested from her tight space in the corner.

A cameraman was filming it all, a light shining over his lens. Chance held on to Jenny's hand, telling her to breathe.

Corabelle kneeled on the floor close to Chance.

I squished myself along the side with the evil EMT, past the cameraman.

"This is crazy," I said to Jenny.

She flashed a pained smile.

"It'll pass in a second," Corabelle said. "We're five minutes apart now."

"Still plenty of time," Darion said from the door as he yanked it shut. "Would you like me to check you?"

"Who are you?" the EMT demanded.

He saluted her. "Dr. Darion Marks. St. Anthony's."

The EMT mumbled something under her breath.

"It will be fine," Darion said.

Jenny's breath began to slow. "Let's not give the cameraman a show," she said. "We can start again."

"What did we miss?" I asked.

"Dylan's been rambling about everlasting love," Chance said.

"This is my finest work," Dylan said, flashing his megawatt smile. He was dressed in black leather pants and a gray silk vest. His hair was perfection, falling over one eye in just the right way. He looked like a rock star, no doubt about it.

"Let's get on with it," Jenny said. "We're probably getting close to the hospital." The ambulance lurched forward, and all the occupants tried to grab something steady to keep their places.

"Absolutely," Dylan said. "Do you, Jenny, take Chance to be your lawfully wedded husband, for better or worse, in sickness and in health, for richer or poorer, from this day forward, till death do you part?"

Jenny looked up at Chance. His face was only inches from hers. "I do," she said.

"And do you, Chance," Dylan went on, "take this lovely lady Jenny, who is laboring so hard for your child, even while attending your concert, as your lawfully wedded wife, for better or worse, and you'll probably make it worse, in sickness and in health, and be ready for a lot of sickness with a kid around, for richer or poorer — speaking of rich, is your recording done yet?"

"Dylan!" several people said at the same time.

"Right, right, for richer or poorer, from this day forward, till death do you part?"

Chance leaned in close to Jenny and pressed his forehead against her temple. "I do."

"By the power vested in me by the Internet, I now pronounce you husband and wife," Dylan said, with a wave of his arms that almost smacked both Darion and the cameraman. "Now kiss this bride before she pops out your kid!"

Jenny turned her face to Chance and he kissed her softly, tenderly. The light from the camera cast a soft glow over both of them.

Everyone in the ambulance cheered. Then Jenny started to groan. "Here comes another one!" she said.

"Four minutes," Corabelle said, her face colored blue from the light of her phone. She had a stopwatch app open.

The ambulance rolled to a stop. Darion peered out the back window. "We're here." He flipped the latch on the door and pushed it open.

Darion jumped out, then Dylan, then the cameraman. He continued to film as the rest of us filed out. Finally, the glowering EMT began unlocking the stretcher so they could get it out the back.

Darion ran up to the sliding glass doors and approached the intake nurse. I was glad we were on familiar turf. I hadn't realized Jenny's obstetrician worked out of the same hospital as Darion. I should probably have asked more questions, been a better friend. But babies were tough territory for me. Like Corabelle, I'd avoided contact with infants or people whose domestic bliss made them likely to pop one out anytime. But here we were.

The male EMT let down the wheels to the stretcher and locked them in place. They rolled Jenny out. She was in the throes of another contraction, panting. When Chance could get next to her again, he took her hand and kissed it.

For the first time since we'd intercepted the ambulance, my throat tightened. Jenny's baby was coming. We'd have a baby among our friends.

I caught Corabelle's eyes. She stood off to the side, her hands clasped tightly together under her chin. Her face mirrored how I felt. Elated. Excited. Fearful. But also, for us, in agony as we considered what had never been.

4

JENNY

"What do you MEAN I don't get any drugs?" I didn't think I could yell that loud, particularly since my insides felt like a car getting crunched into a bundle of twisted metal. But apparently, I could.

The OB on call had a mean face, big nasty eyebrows, and a triangle goatee. He looked like an evil overlord. "You're too close to delivery for it now," he said.

I turned to send a pleading look at Chance. "Can you please call Dr. Jamison's office again?"

Chance looked like he was about to argue that there was no point, but thought better of it and pulled out his phone.

The Evil One looked even more menacing now. Yeah, I didn't want him. I'd made that clear. He patted my knee patronizingly. "You're in good hands. The nurses will let me know when it's time. It won't be long." He turned and strode out the door.

His words made me even more furious. I needed to pull rank.

"Tina!" I called out.

She stood up from a chair in the corner. Thankfully the birthing suites were large. Corabelle was still here, and of course Chance. Dylan and his cameraman had gone back to the concert.

Tina leaned on the bars on the side of my bed. "What's up, baby girl?"

I grabbed her arm. "Can Darion deliver babies?"

I could see her trying not to laugh. "Sure," she said. "But they're going to have a whole team in here when it's time, since the baby is early. You'll probably have to go with Dr. Schlock."

God, that name. That goatee. That attitude. Anything but that. "They said the baby was fine. Lungs working, weight great. Will it really be that bad?"

A nurse came in on the last question. "I'm going to be here for the duration now," she said. "Doc says you're close and we're going to move you into pushing position during the next contraction."

I could already feel it coming on. They were super close together now that we'd gotten through admitting and a quick sonogram to check the baby's lungs. The radiologist had almost told us the gender, but Corabelle managed to cut him off. She was good at knowing what people were about to say.

I looked down at my belly, strapped with a gizmo that monitored the baby's heart rate and the length of the contractions. A blue sheet was covering me below that, not that it mattered. Half the hospital had been all up in my business from the moment I got rolled in.

Seriously, why did anybody care if Britney flashed her parts getting out of a limo when you could see a million of the same in any maternity ward?

I started panting without even wanting to. God, this was ridiculous. Then all my thoughts sort of got erased as the pain took over. A long guttural wail came out of me. I'd normally be humiliated at my lack of control over myself, but whatever. I had no choice but to succumb to whatever the hell my body wanted to do.

Somewhere among all the bludgeoning of my midsection, I felt a deep heavy spreading sensation. I pictured literal jaws opening down below, a big metal mouth groaning in protest, rusted or something, refusing to budge. The image was traumatizing and I had to scream to make it go away.

"You're doing great, honey," the nurse said. "Dad, help her sit up and give her some support."

Chance tried to maneuver me into the position we'd practiced in class, but I elbowed him in the gut. Serves him right for getting me in this damn mess. One damn condom. Who only carries one damn condom?

I might have said that out loud. I wasn't super sure what was real anymore. Everything was hazy, pain making all the edges fuzzy.

"WHERE ARE THE DRUGS?!!!" I shouted.

The nurse peered under the sheet again. I wanted to kick her. Hell, we might as well have the Google car do a drive-by and snap a shot for the satellite feed. I had a bad feeling my privates were about to rival the Grand Canyon.

"Time to push," the nurse said. "Push to ten. Count with me. One, two, three, four…"

I couldn't pay attention to numbers. The pain I felt before was nothing compared to the sharp, burning sensation down below. Now I wanted to go BACK to just the contractions. That was paradise compared to this.

I couldn't push anymore, because that made the burning worse. "I can't," I said. "It's like a million firecrackers going off down there!"

I don't think anyone understood what I said. Chance sat behind me, helping me stay in position, one hand squeezing mine. My hair was everywhere. I had a concert 'do, not something for birthing babies. Sweat was making my styling products run down my face. I could taste hair spray and chalk.

This had to be the worst day ever.

The contraction slowed down, but before I could even catch my breath or complain about something, it started up again. "This suuuuucks!" I managed to get out. Who was supposed to handle this? I was never having another baby. Never never never.

Darion popped into the room. Between gasps, I managed to say, "Pleeeease handle this instead of the Evil Overlord."

I could tell nobody knew what I was talking about. I wanted to hit something in frustration, but instead kept one fist full of sheet and the other in a death grip on Chance.

"Are we crowning?" Darion asked the nurse.

I had no idea what he meant.

"Almost," she said. "I'll call Dr. Schlock in a moment."

I saw Darion smirk at the doctor's name and felt a little better for like a nanosecond.

"Let's push, Jenny," the nurse said. "To ten. One, two…" She faded out faster this time, the pain blasting out everything else.

I felt so exhausted. The contraction slowed, then came right back again.

"Now we're getting there," the nurse said.

"You want me to page him?" Darion asked.

"Sure," she said.

"No!" I shouted, although it sounded like a strangled gasp.

They looked at me. "I want Darion," I said.

The nurse shook her head. "Dr. Marks isn't authorized to deliver except in emergencies," she said.

I wanted to say, "This is an emergency," but the nurse started counting again. Darion backed off and typed something on his phone.

But in seconds, the most amazing, wonderful face in the world showed up. Dr. Jamison. He wore dark blue scrubs and a light blue cap. His kind eyes lit on me and Chance and he smiled.

I started crying. Big huge tears. Snot bubbled from my nose.

"You're doing great, baby," Chance said. "It'll be better now that Dr. Jamison is here."

"I see you decided to speed things along, Jenny," Dr. Jamison said. "Always trying to be more efficient."

I couldn't answer, just boohooed through the pain.

"Where are we?" he asked the nurse.

She rattled off centimeters and other stuff I couldn't pay attention to. I was just glad she wasn't counting, wasn't making me push.

"Breathe, baby," Chance said. He wiped my face with a tissue.

"Why…didn't…I…get…drugs?" I blubbered.

Dr. Jamison reached over and took my hand, squeezing it. "I'm so sorry you went into labor so quickly. After a certain point we turn down the medication so you can push, and you were already almost there when you arrived."

Finally, someone who was willing to actually explain things.

Still, huge, hot tears slid down my face. I felt three years old.

"You're doing great," Dr. Jamison said, and took the nurse's position between my knees. He glanced down, then back up at the nurse. "Bring in the team. We're crowning."

I wiped my eyes with the back of my hand and gripped Chance again.

Dr. Jamison pushed the sheets back so I could see my own knees. Behind him, the doors opened and two female nurses pushed a contraption inside, a crib with something over the top.

I couldn't focus on that because now I didn't need anybody counting to push. My body was pushing without me.

"Help it along if you like," Dr. Jamison said. "But you're nearly there."

Chance pressed on my back to help me see. The pain was a blur now, like I'd gotten used to it, or someone had shot some crazy drug into me that made everything soft. The edges of everything had a sort of glow.

I looked down. The doctor's gloved hands applied pressure around a strange white bulge. Nothing looked anything like I was used to. I was confused about my own body parts, and what I was seeing.

I closed my eyes. That was easier, except then the pain moved forward in prominence. I opened them again.

The doctor barked some command. I sensed all the people moving into position and a nurse closed in.

A new sort of pain ripped through me, hot as a poker, searing.

"Here he comes," Dr. Jamison said. "Head's coming through."

Chance leaned over. I could feel the heaviness of his body. I tried to look, tried to concentrate, but everything was fuzzy.

The white bulge moved out, and I finally realized this was the baby's head. The doctor turned him slightly, and I could see a nose.

"One more good push, Jenny," he said.

I bore down, ready for this to be done, to be able to see the baby. My jaw ached from clenching it, and my whole body felt wrung out. But I pushed. I counted in my head.

Then I looked again.

One shoulder came out, then the other. Then the baby slid out without any sort of struggle. The cord dangled between us, covering the important parts.

Was this a boy or a girl? I wanted to ask, but couldn't catch my breath.

Then Dr. Jamison pushed the cord aside, and I could see. The baby was a girl. A girl!

One of the nurses stuck a bulb in the tiny mouth and sucked something out. The baby began to cry then, a strangled little sound. Then it got louder and louder. A nurse wrapped her in a blanket and laid her on my belly. I put my hand on her back. She was here.

I looked up at Chance in wonder. He couldn't stop staring at the baby, his daughter. His little girl. I leaned my head on his shoulder.

"You want to cut the cord?" Dr. Jamison asked.

"Sure," Chance said. He pushed pillows behind me and moved down to my knees.

I didn't care what they were doing down there. I just kept my focus on the baby, who had given up on crying, conked out on my stomach.

After a moment, Chance stood and the nurse lifted the baby

higher, to my chest. "Hold her for a moment," she said. "Then we need to assess her. She's early."

This made me panic, and I pulled her tight. She looked so perfect and tiny. I didn't think anything could be wrong.

Chance kissed the top of my head and held the baby's tiny hand between his fingers. "She'll be all right," he said.

The nurse leaned in and took her. I felt cold and empty as her body left mine. I started weeping, and Corabelle rushed forward. "You're okay," she said. "She's okay."

The two nurses and a man in scrubs surrounded the plastic crib. I couldn't see what they were doing. I nudged Chance. "Go watch," I said.

Tina was snapping pictures with her phone. Thank goodness.

My mom was going to be devastated that she wasn't here. I had to call her. There was no help for it, as she wasn't even in San Diego right now. But she'd get here as soon as she could. And so would Dad. They were grandparents.

And of course Mrs. McKenzie, Chance's mom.

I scooted the pillows back and lay against the bed. I was exhausted and elated at the same time. Everything surged in me. I couldn't rein in my emotions.

The man in scrubs nodded and came over. "The baby looks just fine. Her Apgar was 7, which is really good for her gestational age."

"Do I get to keep her in here?" I asked.

"We're going to take her for just a few minutes to clean her up and check her lungs, then we'll bring her right back."

"I'm going," I said, and tried to pull my legs out of the stirrups.

"Not yet," Dr. Jamison said. He was still in position at the end of the bed. "We still have some tidying up to do."

"I'll go," Chance said. "Corabelle, you'll stay with her?"

"No!" I said. "Corabelle, go with the baby. You'll know what's happening."

"I'll stay with her," Tina said. She sat on the edge of the bed and squeezed my arm. "Let us know what's going on."

"This is all standard procedure," Dr. Jamison said. "If something was going wrong, there would be a lot more people in here."

They rolled the crib out. The crib with my baby. Mine! I tried to calm down, but my breathing was rapid. I didn't want her out of my sight. "I'm scared," I said.

Darion came over to the bed. "I'll go too," he said. "I can text Tina what is going on."

Dr. Jamison nodded. "Lots of people in your corner, Jenny. It's going to be fine."

He finished whatever he was doing and pulled down the sheet. He lifted my knees out of the stirrups and laid them gently back on the bed. The relief was so great to be out of the position that I almost cried out.

"Rest a little if you can," he said. "You're going to be up a lot in the next few weeks." He patted my arm. "You did great."

"She's really okay?" I asked.

"Seven is a great score. Her lungs were good. They'll make sure."

I nodded. I was so tired. So tired.

Tina found a wet washcloth by the bed and pressed it to my head. "Darion knows these people," she said. "He'll make sure it's all done right."

I reached up and pressed the cool cloth against my eyes.

Holy hell, I'd done it.

5

CORABELLE

I followed the team down the hall from the birthing suites to the NICU. Chance strode behind them, his face tight with concern.

I knew what Jenny was feeling right now, watching your baby get rolled away from you. My heart squeezed and I tried to put the memories of my own baby, Finn, out of my mind.

But everything around me brought it back. The door decorations with the streamers and teddy bears in blue or pink. The echoes of crying babies and hushed conversations of family. Even the shhrrrr sound of the wheels on the smooth waxed floor.

As we approached the glassed wall of the NICU, I stopped dead. I couldn't go in there. No way. My heart hammered fiercely, and my palms sweated. Through the window I could see the rows of cribs, mothers rocking in padded chairs.

I felt faint. I realized I was holding my breath. I hadn't done that in ages, my old coping strategy to make myself go unconscious when life got too hard. I thought I was better, but I could see now that no matter how happy my current life got, my past never left me.

The nurses pushed the crib with Jenny's baby between the sliding doors, but Darion stayed with me. "They won't let you in right now anyway," he said.

I nodded, focusing on my breathing. Air in, air out. Even though we were outside the windows and couldn't hear any sounds from inside the NICU, my ears roared with the helicopter chh chh chh of a ventilator. I could picture Finn lying in his crib, that terrible sound the only thing we heard for the seven days he lived.

It was the most horrible noise imaginable, although there was one that was worse.

The silence after the machine was turned off.

My eyes started to show polka dots. I had forgotten to breathe again. I sucked in a great gasp of air.

Darion took my arm. "Corabelle, are you okay?" he asked.

I had to act normal. "You can go in, right?" I asked, forcing my voice steady. "Jenny wanted us to watch over the baby."

"I think I'll stay here with you." He moved farther down the window, to another room where babies were cleaned and weighed. A set of grandparents were there, watching a newborn girl get washed. The father was inside, taking pictures and beaming.

Moments I never got. Remorse bubbled over. I thought I was handling Jenny's pregnancy fine. She was my best friend. I was happy for her. But all the resentment and bitterness and jealousy I'd held in for nine months suddenly spilled out.

Why was she getting a baby and I wasn't?

She hadn't even known Chance's last name when it happened!

Why did everything bad have to happen to me?

Darion's hand pressed into my back, and I realized I was panting. "Do you need to take a little break from all this?" he asked.

I didn't answer. There was nothing I could say. If I walked away, it meant I couldn't manage, couldn't control my feelings. If I didn't, I would continue to suffer, to nurse all these negative, terrible emotions.

"I'm sure Tina is having a hard time too," Darion said. "Sometimes I come through this ward and see her here, forehead against the glass."

I had no idea she did that. "Why does she torture herself that way?" I asked.

"She pushed her pain aside for a long time. Now she knows she has to actually work through it to get to the other side."

Working through it. I wondered if I had done that. If Gavin had. I wasn't sure what that really meant. Mostly you just kept on going.

I looked back through the window. A nurse was dressing the other baby in a white long-sleeved onesie and pink-striped hat. The infant tightened her eyes every time her father flashed another picture.

"Should you go check on Jenny's baby?" I asked.

"They didn't call in a specialist," Darion said. "I think they'll clean her up and let her go back. She'll have monitors to make sure everything's okay. The first night is the most critical."

He turned and led me away from the window to an alcove with a waiting area. I sat down on a gray cushioned chair, and he settled across from me. I focused on anything that would take my mind off the babies. Darion's dark hair curled across his forehead, a little longer than it was when he and Tina first met. His eyes were concerned. I noticed the paint spatters across his pale yellow T-shirt. "What were you doing when Jenny called?" I asked.

"Painting a portrait," he said. He looked down at his shirt. "These are my art duds."

They'd dropped everything to come be with Jenny. That's what friends did. They didn't put themselves first. I had to pull myself together, for her.

"Go on, then, and check on the baby," I said. "I'll let Gavin know what is going on. Then we can update Jenny if Chance can't get back to the room anytime soon."

Darion stood up. "You sure you're okay?"

I nodded. "It's not easy, but it's been five years. I can manage it." I smiled up at him as convincingly as I could. "Besides, it will be your and Tina's turn next."

"Maybe. I have to convince her first." He turned toward the NICU. "Is Gavin going to come?"

"Yes. He was playing pool with Mario tonight while I went to the concert, nothing important."

Darion headed toward the NICU entrance. I picked up my phone as if I was going to send a text, but as soon as he was out of sight, I set it down again.

The past hour was a total blur. When we were busy, trying to follow Jenny's commands for the wedding and the ambulance ride and the doctor, I was fine. But now, I could barely contain my emotions.

The image of Jenny's baby coming out and that tiny first cry was like a stab to my heart. Finn hadn't cried. I hadn't known that he should have. I was so young, just seventeen. I had no idea how wrong everything could go.

Within minutes of the birth, Gavin had taken off with the NICU crew, just like Chance. And then he'd come back alone.

I leaned my head back on the chair. An older couple passed carrying balloons and flowers. Happy family, meeting their new member. More things I hadn't known.

Might never know.

Gavin had gotten a vasectomy in the dark days after Finn died. Sometimes I tried to imagine the places he had been, the horror that was his life after he ran. But I knew that awfulness. I had been there, alone too, and not by choice.

Even though we'd found each other again, we might never get back to that place of hope. The vasectomy reversal process was expensive and didn't always work. Gavin had gone to some illegal hack shop in Mexico for the procedure. No telling what they had done to him.

And then there was money. I was in school. Gavin was pulling every shift at the garage that Bud would give him, down to just one night class this semester. It took everything we had to manage classes and work. Having a baby anytime in the near future seemed hopeless.

Chance came out of the NICU with Darion. I jumped out of my chair. "What's happening?" I cried. "Where's the baby?"

"She's fine," Chance said. "They're about to bring her around to the window for cleaning. I was going to see if Tina wanted to take pictures."

I looked up at Darion for confirmation.

"She's six pounds, which isn't a lot, but on target for her gestational age," Darion said. "Everything looks really good."

I turned back to the window. They were rolling the other baby girl out of the room with her father. "So, she'll come here?" I asked.

"Yes, in just a minute or two," Chance said.

"I'll go fetch Tina," Darion said.

I stood at the window, fingers pressed against the glass. Darion took off down the hall and Chance got buzzed back into the NICU.

The room was empty, a few clear plastic cribs waiting under heat lamps for their next occupants. My throat tightened again. I felt like a seesaw, swinging up and down and down and up. Control, then losing it. Happy for Jenny, miserable for myself. How did anyone bear something like this?

I remembered I had never texted Gavin and wrote a quick message.

Jenny had the baby. A girl. Small but healthy. We're at the hospital if you want to come up.

He wrote back quickly.

Be right there. You holding up okay?

I held on to the phone for a moment. Tell him the truth, or play it off? I opted for truth.

Struggling not to fall apart, actually.

Coming now. I won't let you go through this alone.

I leaned my forehead against the glass, cool and smooth. The halls were quiet on a Saturday night.

I closed my eyes and let myself pretend that I was waiting on my own baby, that the sounds and smells around me were part of a world that waited for me. In just a moment, the newborn would be rolled into the room, and my parents would snap pictures and smile.

Calmness flowed through me, a quiet joy. I would get there, somehow. We'd find a way.

A clatter on the other side of the window startled me and I opened my eyes.

The back door to the room had opened, and a nurse in pink scrubs rolled a crib into the room. The paper sign taped to the top had Jenny's last name, GILLESPIE, written at the top, crossed out, and then Chance's last name, MCKENZIE, written below. I had to smile. Chance knew he had to get that right or Jenny would have a fit. The name change was the whole reason for her rushed ambulance wedding.

The nurse had just positioned the baby near the window when Darion and Tina turned onto the hall. I waved my arm to hurry them along. "She's here," I called out. "They are about to clean her up."

But Tina didn't rush. I could see the mixed emotions on her face, ones that mirrored exactly how I was feeling. I had gotten seven days with my Finn. Tina had gotten only a few hours.

When she reached the window, I took her hand. "You doing okay?" I asked.

She shrugged. "Probably about as well as you," she said.

Her mascara was smudged. Like Darion, her long button-down shirt was spattered with paint, untucked over rainbow tights. Her signature short twiggy ponytails made her seem like a character on a kids' television show. But her expression was tight. She wasn't bothering to fake it.

She squeezed my fingers and let go, raising her cell phone to take shots of the baby. "They don't have a name picked out," she said as she clicked.

"It'll come," I said.

Tina lowered her camera to watch them unwrap the baby, whose feeble cry quickly ramped up into an all-out wail. "With Jenny, who knows what it might be," Tina said. "She's got the celebrity bug, so she'll probably go with something crazy like Apple or Rainbow or Celery."

This made me laugh. "Celery?"

"Or Rhubarb. Actually, don't mention Rhubarb because she would totally go for it."

Darion leaned his forearm on the glass. "Chance doesn't have a say?"

"That boy is totally steamrolled by the force of Jenny," Tina said.

It was true. Chance was a southern gentleman to the core, and he was no match for his whip-cracking fast-talking California media-junkie wife.

"They've really struggled with how to incorporate Hannah and Bryan into the name," I said.

"Middle name, for sure," Tina said. "It's just too soon to be naming her after the sister. It hasn't even been a year."

Chance's sister had died shortly after he and Jenny met.

"They'll do what they think is right," I said.

The nurse passed a wet cloth over the baby, whose face was bright red from crying. Chance looked like he was about to collapse from stress over watching her misery.

"This is going to be difficult, isn't it?" Tina asked, her voice soft. She lowered her phone. "I already want to smash something."

Her tone made tears spring to my eyes. "We're holding up so far," I said.

Darion cleared his throat. "This is probably the worst part," he said. "From now on, Jenny will have the hard work of managing the baby, and that isn't very glamorous. She's going to be jealous of you most of the time."

Neither of us answered. Maybe he was right, maybe not. But as we watched Jenny's baby get swaddled into her blanket like a burrito and settle down, and as Chance got his opportunity to pick up the baby, love all over his face, Tina silently handed the phone to Darion to take over the photographs.

Then we both simply had to turn away. Some things were just too hard to be borne.

6

TINA

When Chance left the nursery with the baby to head back to Jenny, I peeled away from Corabelle and Darion to stop by my art therapy room. I'd had enough of babies and happy-freaking-joy. I needed some downtime. Alone.

The lights were out in the classroom, and I left them that way as I stepped inside. The glow filtering in from the observation window was enough to provide a soft illumination on the low desks, the paints and clay and tiny easels.

Almost all my art therapy classes were children now. The program had grown in popularity, and we were in the process of hiring a second therapist to expand the number of classes for adults. The main roadblock had been space. Hospitals were notoriously low on empty rooms. Even my favorite Surgical Suite B, which had been used for storage — and sometimes for me and Darion— was now in operation.

I sat at my desk to pull myself together. I wanted to erase all the images from the last two hours from my head. Not the wedding. That had been hilarious. But the labor and birth. And the baby in that blasted room, getting cleaned and primped for her return to Jenny. I felt sick with bitterness. I wanted to wallow in it, dive headfirst into the sludge until it dragged me under.

My phone buzzed. I didn't look at it right away, resting my hot forehead on my cool wrists. Even though my scars were pale and barely noticeable now, I felt the throb of the lines as if the wounds were fresh.

For the first time in years, I heard the siren call of the razor blade. To damage myself. To bear visible scars.

Jesus. How far we can fall so fast. It was just a baby. Jenny having one didn't change anything about me or my past. I needed to get my shit together.

I picked up my phone. It was Darion, asking if I was all right. I typed off a quick note that I was going to visit Albert and that I could catch a ride back to the condo. He said he'd wait. He always had something to do up at the hospital, and now that his sister was staying part-time with their dad, we had more time to overwork ourselves to an early grave. We needed to get that habit in check.

At some point we needed to plan the wedding. Get a life. Make one. Our painting together tonight was one of the things we were doing to ensure we had some life balance.

The chair rolled away from me as I stood. My body blocked the light from the window, leaving half my desk in shadow. I shifted so I could see my mermaid sculpture, one Albert had made for me. He was one of my first art therapy patients, an elderly artist with Parkinson's.

I'd been working with him for several weeks when I

discovered that he was a famous artist who had been reported dead from suicide by his assistant, and he'd been paying someone to keep his Wikipedia entry updated with that erroneous information ever since. When I almost lost my job at the hospital due to my lack of qualifications, he endowed my position with the stipulation that I could work there as long as I wanted.

He was my mentor, and these days, one of my best friends.

But the end was coming. I headed out of the art therapy room and to the elevator.

For the first months Albert was in the hospital, he could still paint and sculpt on good days, when the meds were working on his muscle tremors.

But his decline had begun to accelerate, and no cocktail of Levodopa/Carbidopa seemed to really help anymore. His weakness and trembling meant he mostly lay in bed, his ladylove by his side, and talked me through my problems with my current art projects.

His ward was quiet and dim. Regina, the charge nurse, glanced at me and nodded as I passed. When I arrived at Albert's door, I eased it open gently to make sure I didn't wake him if he was sleeping.

Layla was long gone this late, so Albert was alone in the room. I could see her simple touches even in the semidarkness. A dried flower wreath over the bed. A crocheted doily beneath a hand-painted vase. She was a crafter, an artist who dabbled, as she liked to say.

The two of them had met in my therapy room, and I was more than thrilled to see the late-in-life romance bud between them. Even as we were facing the end, we needed love and hope.

Albert wasn't asleep, and his pale eyes followed me as I

approached. He opened his mouth to speak, but the words didn't come right away. After a couple more attempts, he finally got out "Tina."

I sat on his bed and took his trembling hand. His tremors were extra bad today, his entire hand rocking as if keeping beat to some tribal rhythm. Even my holding it did not calm the spasms. Such a horrible disease. The worst for someone whose lifeblood flowed through his talented fingers. Albert's art had been sold the world over, when he could still make it.

"Jenny had her baby," I said. "A girl."

He almost smiled, but I could see him remembering, and his fingers squeezed around mine. "Sad, then?" he asked.

I nodded. "About the same as if you saw someone butchering one of your famous clowns."

His mouth twisted in a wry smile. "That's…called greeting cards," he managed to get out. "Every day."

"They put your grim little clowns on greeting cards?" I asked.

Another smile. "And calendars…damn agent."

I tried to picture the maniacal characters gracing someone's day planner. I guessed there was a market for anything. They'd made Albert famous enough that he went into hiding. And when his assistant found him with his wrists cut and told the world he had died, he was relieved to be out of the public eye.

He spoke slowly, with great deliberation. "What are you working on?"

"Still the cliff painting," I said. It had been months since I had been inspired to paint my baby, Peanut, at the age he would be now, standing on a cliff over the ocean here in San Diego.

"Perspective right yet?" he asked.

"I'm on attempt number eight," I said with a sigh. His hand felt papery and thin in mine. The tremor ran through his muscles like a heartbeat.

"Just getting started," he said.

I pushed out a rueful laugh. "I know. I've totally let go of the idea that I can do anything worthwhile on the first — or twentieth — try."

"Good girl," Albert said. His eyes drooped, but he forced them open, trying to keep his spark. He really wanted so much more time, so much more life. My heart squeezed painfully.

"I actually tried it inverted just to get the feel for it," I said. "So gloomy and dark that way. Made me think of you."

His mouth twisted as half of it smiled. "Good."

Talking was clearly painful and difficult for him, so I decided to just keep up my end of the conversation. "I got to ride in an ambulance with a rock star, his crew, Jenny in labor, Corabelle, and a pissed-off EMT while Jenny and Chance got married en route to the hospital."

One of his eyebrows lifted.

"Darion and I were painting." I gestured to my spattered shirt with my free hand. "But we caught up with the ambulance and jumped on."

Albert's eyes glittered. He was enjoying the story.

"She literally refused to get off the ambulance until they were legal. That girl is so nuts." I rolled my eyes. "The baby is early, so she's small, but apparently everything is okay."

"Good," he said. "But you?"

I let out a sigh. "I'm keeping up appearances. The way you spend your days is the way you spend your life." I kept my focus on the wreath over his head, refusing to meet his gaze. "I'm trying to spend them happy."

He shook my hand from side to side until I turned back to look at him. "Process," he said. "Feel."

Albert was one person I tried to always be honest with. "I don't want to feel those things too much. The path is slippery and dark. It's a long fall." I flipped my wrists up, even though you couldn't see the fine lines in the gloom. He would know.

He let go of my hand and wrapped his trembling fingers around my wrist. They were warm where they had been in contact with mine, chilly where they had not. It didn't escape me how important that was. Holding on to another person is what kept us alive and strong. Otherwise we would struggle in the chill of solitude.

"You won't go there again," he said.

"I don't know that," I said. "I feel like I'm always one bad day away from the worst."

His eyes bored into mine. He didn't have to say anything. We'd had this conversation before.

"I know. I have Darion. And Corabelle and Jenny. And my work." I glanced around his room. "But I also have this black hole inside me." I couldn't really put into words what I felt. But I could picture it. It always floated just outside my vision. I was too frightened to look directly at it. And I would never paint it, never make it real.

His voice had more strength when he said, "Life is dancing around the blackness."

I wanted to picture this. I tried to see myself, striped tights, spriggy ponytails, cavorting on the edge of the blackness, a colorful sprite laughing in the face of the siren call of despair.

But I wasn't sure I could do it. I wasn't sure I would ever be able to do it.

"Go see your friend's baby," Albert said. "Paint your pain. Leave it on the canvas. Remove it from your soul."

He closed his eyes and his hand slid from my arm. His breath escaped in a long sigh. I squeezed his fingers one more time and stood.

Albert had been saying the same things as long as I knew him. Paint my pain. I'd gone through so many canvases, so much drawing paper, so many tubes of oils.

But maybe everyone was right. I'd left that dark hole on the periphery of my vision. I hadn't even stared into it, much less danced in its shadow.

But now the life I thought I'd lead was right in front of me. Jenny. Her baby. Darion would want a family eventually. I had no idea how I could face the idea of losing another one.

Just thinking about it, I was quite sure I'd rather stare into the depths of the pit. At least it was familiar.

7

JENNY

Motherhood was a piece of cake.

My dad put away the leftover casserole in our fridge, which was stuffed with food my mother's friends had brought over.

Mom rocked the baby in the corner of the living room. The glider was new, a gift from my old boss Frankie. The hot-pink chenille fabric with little silver threads running through it made it the most fabulous piece of furniture I could ever have imagined.

My phone buzzed. I glanced down at it. The stupid old hospital administrator again. For some crazy reason, you weren't supposed to check out without giving your baby a name. I argued until I was blue in the face that you couldn't rush a decision of this magnitude. I had to get the right baby vibes. Little Miss had to show me her personality.

The *last* thing I wanted to do was saddle a *Mavis* with a name like *Penelope*. Or an *Anastasia* with *Jane*.

So I had sort of left. With the forms.

Which apparently was some big deal.

So what?

I mean, it wasn't like taking my time was a crime. What did they expect me to do? Toss any old name on the paper? Forever?

"She's asleep," Mom said, crossing the room. "Shall I put her down?"

I nodded. We'd been home four days. Mom did the laundry. Dad managed the kitchen. Chance had been assembling the outrageous number of contraptions required to keep the baby happy and settled. Swing. Bassinet. Crib. Changing table. And some stuff I couldn't fathom actually using, like this play thingamajig with silver bars and hideous half-baked animal shapes in black and white. It looked like baby jail.

I kissed the baby's warm, soft cheek. She smelled of milk and Dreft detergent. Mom carried her away and I settled back on the sofa. Yes, motherhood was just fabulous.

Dad came back in the room. He wore trim jeans and a button-down shirt rolled up to his elbows. His hair was just now really starting to show its gray. Perfect timing for a grandpa. "I'm going to head back to the hotel," he said. "Got some work things to handle before I fly home tomorrow."

"Okay, Daddy." I hated to see him go. He'd been great manning the kitchen. Hopefully Chance would take that over. My girl parts still felt like they'd been bludgeoned by a meat tenderizer.

"I'll be by in the morning before I'm off." He leaned down and kissed my head. "You're doing great, princess."

"Thank you, Daddy," I said.

Mom came back in the room. "See you tomorrow, Dennis," she said. I knew the two of them had been playing nicey-nice for my benefit. For two people who hadn't seen each other much in the past ten years, they were doing pretty well.

Babies brought out the best in people.

When Dad had gone, Mom sat next to me on the sofa. "Jenny, I heard from work yesterday, and I need to go put in a few hours tomorrow," she said. "I'll be back in the afternoon."

A little tendril of panic shot through me. "But Daddy's leaving too."

She patted my arm. "I know. It will just be a few hours. It will give you and Chance a little time with the baby."

"But I'm not ready." My face flushed. Chance didn't know a blessed thing about the care of the baby.

Actually, neither did I. My mother handled all the diapers and the changing. I just did the boob thing, which luckily had gone pretty well so far.

"You'll be fine," she said. "I'm going to catch a little shut-eye now in case she wakes up in the night. Sleep when the baby sleeps!"

She headed for the nursery. She was spending her nights on a rollaway cot in there for now.

Chance passed her on the way, holding two metal pipes painted bright pink. "Thanks, Mama G," he said. "I'll finish this in the morning."

"Is that the swing?" she asked.

"It will be."

"Good. Jenny loved her swing when she was a baby." She yawned. "I'll bring the baby for a feeding if she needs it."

"I pumped some in the fridge," I said, "so you don't have to wake us."

She nodded. "All right, then." She disappeared down the hall.

Chance set the pipes on the coffee table and sat next to me. "I thought you were having trouble with the pump."

My lips turned down. "I managed to get a little out. But I feel like a big old cow with that thing hooked up to me."

Chance flashed me a wicked grin. "I think it's kinda cool that they have big see-through cones."

I punched him in the arm. He had stripped off his flannel button-down and wore just a thin white sleeveless shirt with his jeans. He looked hot and sexy, like a rock star on his day off.

Meanwhile, I was pathetic in a big blue nightdress with boob panels that were always gaping, and no amount of nursing pads kept the milk stains away.

And I still hadn't fixed my hair color. I was half pink, half dull brown, like a melted double-scoop ice cream cone.

Tears dripped down my face. "Everybody's leaving me tomorrow," I said.

He scooted in close. "They've been a big help, haven't they?" he said. "But we've got to figure this out sometime, don't we?"

I sniffed. "We don't even have a name for her!"

He draped his arm around me. "Well, let's figure it out. What were our contenders?"

"Rain, Phoenix, Lyric, and Jane."

I could feel his stomach tighten as he stifled a laugh. "One of those names is not like the others."

I bumped my shoulder against his chest. "Hush up. We don't know anything about her. She could be very studious and straitlaced."

"Is that the Jane?"

"No, silly, that would be Lyric."

"Wait. Lyric is the studious one?"

"Of course! She'll study music! Like her dad."

"So, which one is the wild, pink-haired minx like her mother?"

"That would be Jane."

"Okay…but isn't that the plainest name?"

"I'm Jenny!"

He had to laugh at that. "Okay. You've got me there. So, who is Rain?"

"She's earthy and calm, like a summer shower."

Chance raised an eyebrow. "You really think either of us could raise one of those?"

"Of course not. Scratch it off the list, I guess." I fingered the hem of the gown. "I am sort of leaning toward Phoenix."

"I could live with that. She rises from her own ashes."

"She'll make a lot of mistakes, but do something magical and wonderful from what she learned."

"Sounds like our girl." He leaned his head against mine.

We sat that way a while, content, the apartment quiet. Everything seemed okay for now. "Phoenix Hannah McKenzie," I said.

"I like it."

"I'll fill out the paperwork tomorrow," I told him. "Get the pencil-pushers off my back."

He slid me down on the sofa. "How are your girl parts feeling?" His body lay next to mine, hard and muscled.

"Don't even think about it, Buster. Two-week minimum. Did you not see what came out of there? Her head was like a squished cantaloupe!"

Chance choked on a laugh. "Point taken."

I pulled on his shirt. "You can kiss the hell out of me, though."

"That I can do." His lips met mine, soft and firm.

I let out a slow sigh as he kissed me long and lingeringly. I felt little pinpricks of interest heading down below, but it was more like a car firing on bad cylinders than anything sexy.

Chance pulled my head against his chest. "Our time will come around again," he said. "Then we can make another one."

I punched his arm. "Don't even talk about it. I'm buying you twenty cases of condoms."

His eyes glittered as he looked at me. "She's beautiful, though," he said. "Like you."

"It'll be a good life," I told him.

"It already is."

~*'`*~

I tearfully waved good-bye to Dad the next morning. Mom had taken off for whatever work was dragging her away from her granddaughter.

I held the baby in the crook of my arm. My shoulder was already killing me. How could something so small feel so heavy?

When Chance closed the door, I asked him if he'd finished the swing.

"Almost," he said. "Give me a half hour."

I didn't want him to leave the room, but I needed that swing. If the baby started fussing, there were only so many boob jobs that would quiet her down.

"Try to hurry," I told him. Mom had said nothing was better

for soothing me when I was little than to be rocked in a swing.

Chance took off for the nursery. I plunked down in the pink glider. The perfect blanket burrito my mother had tied around Phoenix was starting to loosen. I laid her in my lap and tried to fix the ends.

But with a couple tugs, the whole elaborate system of tucks and turns fell open.

Phoenix looked up at me with her slate-blue-gray eyes. She was quiet and alert, her gaze as wise as a baby Buddha.

"I'll just try this again," I told her. "How hard can it be?"

I straightened the small blanket. I crossed one corner over her belly, then the other. But what about the top ones? I tried bringing them down over her shoulders, but this just made a big pile on top.

I put them all back in place and brought the top corners down first this time. Okay, so maybe the bottom ones had to go around the back. I tried turning Phoenix on her side, but she didn't like that and started to cry.

"No no no," I said, picking her up. Her head bobbled a little and her cries got more intense.

Crap! I put my hand behind her neck and lifted her to my shoulder. She quieted, and I sighed relief. She had on a long-sleeved onesie. She would be fine without the burrito blanket.

I felt a warm wetness on my neck and hair. I pulled the baby away.

Gawd, she'd spit up everywhere. It was in my hair and all over my shoulder. A trickle ran down my back.

I set her back in my lap, but she immediately started crying again. I didn't have enough hands to manage her and the mess.

"Chance!" I called out.

He didn't come right away. I picked Phoenix up again and put her on my other shoulder. I could feel spit-up running all down my skin and my gown sticking to my back.

"Chance!" I called again, a little louder.

The noise must have upset the baby, because she started crying even though I already had her up in her favorite position. "Shhh, Phoenix," I said.

This made her cry harder.

I felt hot and sick, sticky and panicked. I fumbled with the slits in the gown, trying to get a boob out to feed her, even though she had just eaten. When I moved her there, though, she turned her head. Her face bloomed red and her cries turned to jagged sobs.

"Chance!" I called out again.

He skidded into the room. "Sorry. Oh, what is that smell?"

"She spit up."

"You sure that's all?" His face contorted.

Now that he mentioned it, I could smell something more. I pressed my hand on the baby's bottom and immediately felt wet. Squishy wet. Phoenix managed to wail even louder, a direct shot to the ear.

"Coming out both ends, I see," Chance said with a chuckle.

"I fail to see what is funny about this," I said. My eyes pricked hot with tears. "My parents have been gone less than five minutes, and she's already thrown up all over me, blown out her diaper, and refuses to eat."

Chance set down the screwdriver in his hand. "Here, I'll take her for a second." But as he reached for me, his phone buzzed.

"Maybe it's your mom? Coming back?" I asked hopefully. Chance's mother had only been down for two days after Phoenix arrived before having to get back to Tennessee for some big church event she was chairing. She promised to come back and help as soon as it was over.

"Actually, it's the producer on the album," Chance said. "And not his assistant. His direct line. I have to take this, babe." He held up one finger. "I'll be right back. I just have to get away from the noise for two secs."

He dashed out the front door.

Oh. My. God.

I clutched the screaming baby to my chest, soggy with every possible bodily excretion. I'd been abandoned by everyone.

And she was only one week old.

8

CORABELLE

The entire kitchen table was covered in pink glitter.

I swiped at my eyes, trying to pull myself together. Jenny's wedding had been converted into a shower for the baby, so I had been given the task of changing all the hanging silver sparkle stars to — what did Jenny call the color? Oh, right. Blushing primrose.

I had to mix six shades of pink and pearl glitter to get the color just right. Which was sort of pointless, as once I put it on top of the old silver color, it shifted and changed depending on the light and how well it stuck.

Jenny texted another picture of the baby every seven seconds, and I was contemplating blocking her. Except I was in charge of this party and she was my best friend.

My utterly clueless, totally self-absorbed, completely maddening best friend.

I scattered another handful of glitter mix across one of the largest stars. I had a bad feeling that my house and car were never going to recover from this infestation of sparkle. I had already caught Gavin tramping through it twice, leaving primrose footprints across the dining room.

I had spread two old sheets on the floor, but I would swear this glitter could fly. It was everywhere.

A fat tear fell squarely on the uppermost point of the star. The drop pushed the color aside, leaving a wet silver circle. Great. I dusted my hands and decided to walk away until I could pull myself together.

This wasn't Jenny's fault. She was as obsessive about baby Phoenix as she had been about her job, and her previous lineup of boy toys, and a dozen other things in the time I had known her. I almost longed for the days when we worked at Cool Beans Coffee Shop and she drove me crazy flirting with anybody who glanced her way.

That was so much easier than this.

Another text buzzed through.

Mom and Dad gone! Chance just left too! Baby crying! Please come help!

I paused, swiping at my eye and feeling the grit of pink glitter on my cheek. Great. First I'm expected to head up her shower. Now I have to help with the baby too?

I tossed my phone on the sofa and plunked down on the floor. There was no doubt about it, I was not handling this well.

I lay back on the carpet and stared at the ceiling. Coats of paint failed to completely conceal the water stains from a previous upstairs tenant's bathtub overflow. Parts of the popcorn ceiling were flat from the damage.

Gavin and I could not seem to get ahead on bills. Despite all the work hours he was putting in and reducing his college load, we were still struggling. My TA position covered only tuition and fees for grad school. With Gavin's young son, Manuelito, around, I wasn't able to put in any time at Cool Beans, although I might be able to get some hours since he was gone with his mother to Mexico.

I felt so tired. Working at the coffee shop didn't appeal to me. I felt completely out of touch with all those undergrads and their whining about grades and parents and dating. I couldn't relate to them anymore, and I found myself wanting to shake them and say, "Talk to me when you have REAL problems!"

The phone buzzed again on the sofa, this time a call. Jenny, most likely. I didn't move. I had papers to grade. Stars to glitter. And only a few hours until I had to head up to campus for a long day.

She was on her own. I loved Jenny, but she had to grow up. Nothing like a baby to make it happen.

I shifted so I could see the framed pictures of Finn. When I moved in with Gavin to a larger apartment, I hung the collage in our living room. There were only a few images. I didn't take a lot in those seven days my baby had lived, since he always looked the same, his eyes covered with a little mask and his mouth taped to a breathing tube. There hadn't been much to see. Nothing ever changed but the time and date on the monitor.

Still, I could admire his stubby little nose. The soft cheeks. His fragile curled-up fingers with the tiny nails. When I'd held him the one and only time, he was so light, like a pile of feathers.

I didn't know how Jenny's baby, Phoenix, felt. I'd managed to avoid holding her, not hard with doting grandparents vying for a turn. Up at the hospital, it had been easy to hold conversations with other adults, averting my eyes.

Now she wanted me over there.

The phone rang again.

Crap. I stood up from the floor and headed for the sofa. Yep, Jenny. I sighed and answered the call.

"Where are you?" Jenny cried. "Chance left me! Everybody left me!"

"What's going on?" I asked. I pinned the phone to my ear with my shoulder and started shoving books in my backpack. I could see where this was going.

"She threw up! Twice! Then her diaper exploded!"

"What are you feeding her?"

"Just the boob!"

"How often?"

Jenny's voice sounded exasperated. I could hear the baby crying close by. "I don't know! Every time she cries!"

"She's still taking it?"

"Not anymore! I can't figure out anything to make her stop and Chance left without fixing the swing!"

I zipped up my bag. "You can just put her in her crib. Clean yourself up. Pull yourself together."

"But she's crying! She'll be scarred for life!"

"Nope. She'll probably fall asleep. Did you get her cleaned up?"

"Yes, sort of. It was really sticky."

Geez, didn't Jenny understand this was what motherhood was like? That messes and crying were what babies did?

"Please say you're coming," Jenny said. "I'm going out of my mind."

I glanced at the clock on the wall. "I only have a couple hours until class," I said.

Jenny's breath rushed out, making a shhhhrrrr sound on the phone. "Thank you, Corabelle," she said. "You're the best."

I clicked off the call. The abandoned pink star sat in a sparkling heap on the table. Bits of glitter all over the carpet caught the light. I'd tracked a fair amount out of the dining area myself. I couldn't help but think of the contrast between what Jenny wanted for herself — the perfect pink stars and beautiful party — and what she was going through. Diapers and spit-up and feeling panicked and alone.

Definitely time for her to face reality.

~*'`*~

When I got to Jenny's, she looked more composed than she had seemed on the phone. She wore a bright pink shirt and sparkly gray sweatpants. I tried not to notice the damp spots where her nursing pads weren't quite up to their job.

"The baby fell asleep," Jenny said. "I didn't think it would ever happen."

"Oh, good," I said. Even better if I didn't have to hold or rock her. I'd been stressed about it on the drive over. Just seeing the parts of baby furniture scattered around was starting to set off my need to flee.

"I can't believe everyone deserted me," Jenny said. Her hair was done up in an elaborate updo that mostly hid the change in color. She seemed very put together for someone who was so frantic twenty minutes ago. I struggled to squash my annoyance.

"I think a lot of parenting is sink or swim," I said blandly. My mind wasn't on my words now, but on the panic that was rising in me. I hadn't felt this bad when we were up at the hospital. But here, surrounded by the way life should have looked for me, a baby in the crib, a home and family, my chest was getting tight.

Jenny grabbed my hand and led me toward the hall. "Come see her."

My knees threatened to give out. My strongest urge was to pull away, to resist, but I forced myself to follow her down the short hall to the nursery. I had to do this. Jenny wasn't going away. Neither was her baby. This was something I had to face.

The nursery was dim, the curtains drawn. A soft pink glow came from a shaded lamp in one corner. Our shadows crossed the floor inside the rectangle of light from the hall.

The room was in serious disarray, boxes and a half-assembled swing all over the floor. Jenny navigated the mess to the crib. I couldn't see inside due to the ruffled canopy hanging over it.

Jenny pushed the fabric aside. The baby lay on her back, arms up by her head, wearing a pink and blue sleeper with little roses down the front.

My heart hammered painfully in my chest. My throat felt thick and my head thumped. I tried to take a step forward, but stumbled on a screwdriver.

I wanted to walk up and fake it. Admire the baby. Say something encouraging. Jenny was my friend. This was her baby. They would be a part of my life.

But some other force took over. Instead of getting closer, I backed away. I couldn't do it. I kept seeing Finn's crib with its cascade of butterflies flying over it. When I came home from the funeral after Gavin had taken off, alone and flooded with despair, I had destroyed the handmade mobile, piece by piece.

"I-I'm sorry," I said to Jenny. "I have to get to class."

I whirled around, almost ramming into the door frame, and tore through the apartment. I ran and ran, out the door, to my car, wrenching it open and shoving the key in the ignition.

I don't know if Jenny came out. I couldn't look. I just backed out of the spot and sped away from the scene. I could not handle this. It was the life I had once imagined, longed for, and lost. And now it was the one I might never have.

I wasn't sure I could be her friend anymore.

9

TINA

Both Corabelle and Jenny had texted me multiple times since the pink explosion of a baby shower began, but I only glanced at my cell phone with each soft buzz. I had nothing to say.

I wasn't anywhere near the venue where the tortuous event was being held. While I originally was supposed to play a role in this day, my duties as bridesmaid had been fulfilled in the ambulance. Now that the wedding was a baby extravaganza, I had no desire to sit around while people grinned like idiots over giraffe rattles and fuzzy blankets.

The charcoal scraped across my textured sketch pad like a whisper. The drawing of Albert in his hospital bed emerged slowly from the curves and lines. He looked peaceful, his eyes closed, the fingers of one hand positioned as if they surrounded an invisible oil brush. Chaotic gray ringlets framed his face. He definitely still had a full head of hair. His cheeks were deeply lined.

I took my time on the crinkles around his eyes, trying to

imagine a time when he was younger, his wife and daughter still alive, and happy. That must have been when the smile lines formed, before he put on his perpetual brooding expression so often caught in magazine articles or promotional images once he became a famous artist.

I saw a glimpse of that long-lost joy here and there, particularly when Layla was around. She had brought up a painting Albert once made of his daughter. It hung on the opposite wall of his hospital room in real life so he could see it. But in my drawing of him, I moved it to just behind his head, as though she was looking over him. The little girl was three or four, practically bouncing with happiness in a pair of red overalls. A matching headband failed to contain her mass of curly brown hair.

Albert coughed, and I paused, my charcoal still against the page. He didn't wake, though, so I resumed the image, smudging a bit of shadow on the pillow next to his head.

I felt at peace here. Knowing Albert and I shared something so concrete, his daughter and my Peanut, helped keep me calm. My guilt pricked that I was skipping the baby shower without telling anyone, but what was I supposed to say? "Hey, Jenny, I know we're friends, but I'm blowing off your big day because I can't handle it." Right. Best to just shut up.

To tell the truth, I hadn't told Darion either. He had a shift today, so he was here at the hospital. But I knew his routine. I could avoid him. I'd confess later. I just couldn't risk somebody talking me into going. Not worth it.

A nurse slipped in the room. "Asleep?" she whispered.

I nodded. She made a note on her iPad. "I'll hold his lunch tray," she said.

I returned to my sketch. I'd made many of Albert, almost as many as I had of Darion and his sister, Cynthia. Sometimes I drew him painting or sculpting. Other times, it was like this, in a hospital scene. But mostly I liked to capture his expressions. His face always told me so much about him, as much as his art, if I looked closely. He was so haunted. But so eager to impart what he could to me.

While he could.

My breath hitched just thinking about the dark day that surely wasn't far off. Albert slept more and more. Layla helped me track his wakeful periods so I could visit him at those times. Today she was having lunch with a friend, and I was perfectly content to skip the baby shower and sit with him.

I wasn't sure how much longer I would get to.

The door eased open again, and I looked up, expecting that the nurse's message didn't get to the kitchen and Albert's tray had arrived anyway.

But it was Darion.

He stepped inside. He had on a crisp white coat today, which meant he'd been doing some administrative work. He was still relentlessly proper about those things despite my efforts to get him to relax.

His attention turned to Albert for a moment, then he raised his eyebrows at me. I sat stonily, then realized I was busted. Jenny or Corabelle must have messaged him.

I closed the sketch pad and slid the charcoal stick into its slot in my art box. Party over. Or pity party. Whatever this was.

The bag bumped my back as I slung it over my shoulder. I squeezed Albert's arm. He didn't stir.

Darion reached for my hand as I approached. I took it, trying to calm myself with the touch of his cool fingers. We walked silently down the hall until we passed the nurses' desk.

"Let's go to the staff lounge," he said. "It's quiet today."

Saturday afternoons were always a peaceful part of the surgical ward. All the scheduled procedures were done in the morning, and it would be hours before the night activity jumped the ER into gear.

"You're sneaking me into the doctors' den?" I asked.

"Mm-hmm," he said. "Just remember if anyone shows up to act like Chevy Chase and Dan Aykroyd in *Spies Like Us.*"

This did make me laugh. "Doctor, doctor? Doctor, doctor?"

He waved his badge on the door and nudged it open with his shoulder. "Precisely. Only sexier." His voice dropped into a low rumble.

I obeyed. "Doctor, oh, *doctor*," I said with a smile.

"That's more like it," he said.

Now I wondered what he was up to.

We headed inside the lounge. Two sofas lined one wall. In the middle, three large round tables filled the open space. The back wall was all kitchen. A long desk held a couple laptops and charging cables.

A female surgeon in scrubs poured a cup of coffee from one of four carafes near the sink. She gave us a curt nod and headed back out.

"So, this is how the other half lounges," I said.

"Hardly anybody uses this place anymore other than to grab coffee. Nobody has time to sit around and talk shop."

"Damn managed care," I quipped. We'd had this conversation before.

He shrugged out of his white coat. "It is what it is."

Darion was dressed formally as always, white shirt, dress pants, and tie. But he loosened the knot at his throat.

"You going to change?" I asked.

He pulled me close to him. "Undressing isn't necessary on location."

NOW I got it. I glanced at the door. "Are you serious? Right here? In this huge open room where anyone can walk in?"

"They do it all the time on *Grey's Anatomy*." He leaned in and kissed me.

I relaxed into his lips and felt the loosening in my belly, but still. This was an open lounge. Not Surgical Suite B, where nobody ever walked in, well, other than a random custodian.

Still, I didn't break the kiss. I was willing to go where Darion would take me. I was the wild one. He couldn't scare me. And I wasn't convinced he would follow through on this.

Darion slid my bag off my shoulder and dropped it behind him on a table. I could feel everything falling away as I focused on him.

He slid his hands beneath my fuzzy sweater and ran them up my back. "Mmm, braless as usual," he whispered against my lips.

Now he definitely had me. I turned my head just a little. "Deciding to put your career on the line?" I asked against his cheek.

"If doctors got fired for sex on the job, the patients would run the hospital."

I pulled back to look into his eyes. "Dr. Darion Marks, what's gotten into you?"

He shifted a hand around to the front to cup one of my breasts. I sucked in a breath. He said, "It's really more about getting into *you*."

His hands moved down to the backs of my thighs and lifted me up against him.

I allowed my knees to part and wrap around his hips. My arms snaked around his neck so I could hang on.

He nuzzled into the hair over my ear. "That's it."

My heart sped up. Darion was not a risk-taker. This was big. He pulled me firmly against him and took several long strides toward the long counter next to the sink. He set me on an empty spot and shoved the sugar and creamer containers out of his way.

His lips caught mine again. I closed my eyes and quit thinking about where we were, just got lost in the spiraling need that was spinning through my body.

Darion's hands slid up my thighs beneath my skirt. Now the drumbeat was pulsing between my legs, wanting him to move faster, to be bold.

His fingers curled around the lacy strap of my panties. I sucked in a breath against his mouth. "I should ban these," he growled.

"Are we going to need duct tape again?" I asked. Darion had been forced to repair my underwear during a lunchtime tryst when we were first together.

"My skills are better honed," he said. In one quick movement, he lifted me and jerked the panties to my knees.

"Just be glad I prefer to wear skirts," I said.

He tugged the panties down my legs and tossed them on the counter. "I am," he said.

His thumb made a path up my thigh, and I clutched at his neck. When he reached his destination, I lurched against him, desperate for contact. How had he known exactly how to fix me, exactly what to do?

He massaged my nub, making me writhe against his hand. My hips moved with him, reveling in the attention and care he took with each heightening sensation, my tightening need.

I heard his belt jingle and reached down to help him unfasten the buckle. "Now if you would just switch to kilts, we'd be in business," I said, jerking down his zipper.

"We are anyway."

His voice hitched when I found him, lifting him up and out of the boxers.

"Don't take your time," I said, sliding forward on the counter so I was perched on the edge.

His hands spread my thighs wider. I found myself calculating the risk. If someone walked in, they'd see his back, my bare knees. Not much else. My skirt covered us.

It was fine.

Darion shifted forward, and I found him. He reached around to grasp my bottom and drag me onto him.

I gasped as he thrust straight inside. We'd spent so much time being comfortable lately, behind closed doors, in our big perfect bed. This was exhilarating, liberating. Fun.

He reached between us again. He knew what would get to me fast. His thumb pressed against key parts in tight circles. My head felt light, the world falling away. The contact was intense and fierce. He worked me hard with his fingers and his hips rocked against me.

The pleasure radiated out, broad and heavy at first, then splintering into lightning shards. I cried out as it bolted through my body, making me clutch Darion, holding on for dear life.

He buried his face in my neck, his rhythm fast and steady and forceful. My body clamped down on his as the orgasm reached its peak. I felt his body tense, then release, and warmth spread through me. I gasped for breath, coming down with him in degrees.

Darion wrapped his arms around me. "Thank you for indulging me," he said.

I smacked him lightly on the arm. "It was such a terrible inconvenience," I said with a laugh.

He pulled back, his eyes mischievous and merry. "I'm a bad influence on your pristine soul."

"I'll drag you back from hell," I said.

Darion looked down. "I guess we can't stay like this indefinitely."

I followed his gaze to where my skirt was draped over us. One of my shoes had fallen off. "We could always insist we were doing an obstetrical workshop."

This made him laugh hard, his voice cutting through the quiet of the lounge. "Worth a shot."

He pulled back. His hair was disheveled, his shirt wrinkled, and his pants creased. He looked perfect.

I hopped off the counter and retrieved my shoe as he buckled up.

"So, how did you know where I was?" I asked.

"When Corabelle said you weren't at the shower and not responding to texts, I had a good idea." He tried patting his short hair back into place, but just made it worse. I giggled and ran my fingers through it.

"How is Albert?" he asked.

"He didn't wake for me today. I just sketched." I tugged on my spriggy ponytails. One had been knocked askew, and bits were falling out. We were both a mess. I worked on it as I watched Darion, waiting for him to ask why I hadn't gone to Jenny's party. He was supposed to have met me after the shift, and I hadn't even told him I wasn't there.

But he didn't mention it. He picked up his white coat. "I just have the pediatric rounds to go. Lots of them are in your art therapy. You want to come along?"

He wasn't going to ask. I didn't have to say anything. My throat closed up. He got it. He knew me. He really, really knew me.

"Sure," I managed to get out, my voice thick with emotion. I picked up my bag. "I want to see how Henry is doing."

"He's feeling pretty low from his chemo, but he's a cheerful little guy," Darion said.

We headed for the door. "Can we see him first?" I asked.

"No reason why not," he said as he held it open.

The walk through the halls was different from when I'd arrived, dark and heavy from visiting Albert and guilty for skipping Jenny's shower. This time I noticed the new bulletin boards and nodded at passing staff. I was better. This day was passing without a breakdown. Darion had known just what to do.

And what not to try to say.

We were already in the farthest wing of the hospital, almost to Henry's room, when I remembered something.

We'd left the panties on the counter of the lounge.

10

JENNY

Some freaking Thanksgiving.

Everyone out in the living room was drinking and partying. I was stuck in the back bedroom of a rock star's mansion, clumsily trying to get Phoenix to latch on to my overfull boob.

I'd waited too long. I knew it. We'd left the sanctity of my mother's place hours ago and come to a party hosted by a musician on Chance's new record label. Chance was anxious and animated, ready to schmooze.

And I was trying to feed an infant.

I despaired at the milk dribbling onto my glittery skirt. I knew I should have worn something more practical — but this was a party! At least I'd managed to leave Phoenix for three hours yesterday to get my hair fixed.

But neither my fabulous new cotton-candy-pink dye job nor my clever outfit mattered at all since I was stuck in a back room.

Phoenix screwed up her eyes in frustration and wailed. At three weeks old, she'd definitely found her lungs. I searched around for a door to a bathroom, but the only one led me to a closet. I needed a towel to get some of this milk out so my boob was softer for her to latch on to.

Stupid me for waiting so long. I knew I was about to explode. But Phoenix had been asleep, and I hadn't wanted to wake her.

I didn't want to go back out into the hall, where several people were hanging out or hooking up, sprawled on the floors and draped over chairs. I'd had to step over them on my way here.

My shirt was useless for this task, some synthetic stretchy sparkly rayon that wouldn't absorb anything. It scratched me mercilessly anyway. There had to be something here to soak up extra milk.

I wished we were at Dylan Wolf's, where I at least knew people and could ask for help. This was some other guy, some hotshot newcomer who already had a duet with Selena Gomez in the works.

I searched through the closet, but it was empty except for some boxes and a couple sealed suit bags. I looked back at the bed.

I didn't want to do it. But I would have to.

I jerked back the covers and grabbed a pillow. The pillowcase was Egyptian cotton, high thread count. I fumbled to pull it off while holding the howling baby. I had to set her on the bed to get it done. Finally, it came free.

"Sorry, rock-star dude," I whispered as I pressed it against my boob and squeezed. I could see why Phoenix was having trouble. It was hard as a rock.

I worked it for a couple minutes, placating the baby with a

milk-covered finger. The pillow was thoroughly wet before I felt like I'd gotten enough out to try latching her on again.

Thankfully, this time, she went right on. I sank onto the bed in relief. I glanced over at the soaked pillowcase. I wasn't sure what to do with it. No telling what bodily fluids got spilled in back bedrooms at parties like this. I'd just leave it on the corner and let his cleaning people manage it. I had no choice. I wasn't exactly going to tug on his sleeve in the middle of a party and explain that he had breast milk all over his guest-room pillowcase.

Now that my panic was waning, the sounds of the party filtered through the walls. I could hear exactly what I was missing.

Someone had hooked up an electric guitar and was banging out chords. Then a piano filled in a melody. After a minute, somebody sang something and a bunch of people joined in.

Uggh, I was missing it all!

I closed my eyes, trying to find peace with Phoenix and the wonder of motherhood. But I kept picturing the fabulous celebrity-filled Tweets and status updates going on out there. And Chance! He was so oblivious to the whole thing. He probably wasn't taking a single selfie with all the rock gods.

I'd been working with a movie studio the last eight months, running the social media for four of their stars. I knew what it took to stay in the public eye and how to build fan energy for a release. This was a killer opportunity. Tons of the target market was sitting around bored after a day with family, tapping on their phones, and we could be providing them links and pictures to peruse.

Uggh. Come on, baby!

Phoenix was contentedly slurping away. I felt frantic and stuck, wondering if I dared venture out with a baby attached to my boob. I mean, the whole open-breastfeeding movement was a thing. Maybe I could catch a quick shot with some musician PLUS go viral with the earth-mama angle.

My brain whirred. Yes, this would work. I just had to figure out how to arrange this clunky shirt. It was tight and hard to maneuver, hiked up over my boobs right now, revealing the damp cotton maternity bra. I knew I should have made time to go to that trendy shop with the sexy nursing wear!

I headed over to a dresser with a tall mirror. I tugged on the shirt, trying to cover my bra on one side. I despaired over the fleshy bits of my still-deflating stomach that lapped over my skirt. Why did it have to be so tight now? It was shoving skin in all the wrong places.

My eyes pricked with tears. I lifted the skirt higher, trying to avoid exposing too much belly.

That was better. Only the bottom edge of the bra showed. I could hold the baby just the right way to hide that plus any belly bulges. I turned right and left, examining myself in the mirror. Yes, this would do. I wouldn't go viral for all the wrong reasons. That was always my biggest fear. It was one thing to be a big celebrity and get caught in a bad shot or compromising image.

It was another thing entirely to be an average Joe who ended up becoming the next Ermahgerd.

Phoenix was still sucking contentedly. I unzipped my tiny purse and awkwardly tugged out my phone with one hand. I'd have it unlocked and ready for pictures. I'd take some of Chance, of course. Then some selfies.

My heart sped up just thinking about it. This was what I lived for. The baby didn't have to slow me down. I could do this. I could do it better. I mean, who doesn't want an image that also supports a good cause?

I lifted one of Phoenix's cute slippered feet and kissed the toes. "We'll do this together, baby girl," I said. "Take on the world."

When she was back to her perfect position, I opened the bedroom door. The halls were empty now, the raucous singing drawing everyone back into the main living area. I could picture the scene. Rock stars, beautiful people, talent and fame, all having a blast on a holiday weekend.

This was going to be so great!

The end of the hall was a little clogged with people watching, those too shy to push forward. I was not nervous in the least to make my way to the center of the fun.

I found a pocket of space and looked around. Two Grammy Award—winning singers were standing on chairs, singing their guts out. Oh my God! This was perfect! But where was Chance?

I pushed forward again and spotted him sitting on the edge of a shiny black grand piano, more well-known musicians on either side of him. So perfect!

I lifted my cell phone to take a shot. Got it!

I glanced down at the image. Loved it! I didn't want to upload it without thinking carefully about what to say for the best keywords and hashtags. I'd wait for a quiet moment.

Now for my selfie.

I almost fainted when I realized who was next to me. And on the other side. This party had brought out the most amazing pop-star divas. Best selfie op ever.

My hand had started sweating, and my shoulder was throbbing with the effort of holding Phoenix in position. If I could just get the right angle!

I punched the button to switch to the forward camera on my phone. My pink hair filled the frame. I held my arm out as far as it would go, trying to get the baby, myself, and some of the famous people in the shot.

A man jostled me from behind, but I kept my composure, trying to hit the shutter button.

That's when I heard the terrible wail.

I looked down. Phoenix had unlatched, milk all over her face. It dribbled down my exposed boob. I tried to situate her without dropping the phone, but when I moved her again to try to get her back in place, she let out a heart-rending scream.

And that's right when the song ended.

11

TINA

Well, this was this boring.

The hospital holiday party had pretty much nothing going for it other than Darion in a suit. Which was, I would admit, a nice perk.

The actual holidays were long over. This event was always held in January. The increase in hospital workload in late December and at the New Year, plus attempts at vacations and time off, all meant the hospital staff had zero energy to put together something fun.

Not that this was exactly *fun*.

Darion and I sat at a table with some of the other oncologists. The hospital cafeteria had been repurposed for the party. Despite the lights and decorations, it still looked like a cafeteria, in the way a gymnasium is rarely truly transformed for prom.

Three times, one of the wives had redirected the conversation away from clinical trials and new treatment protocols. These guys seriously had no idea how to kick back. Darion was just as bad as the others, but I was used to it. I was equally obsessive about art.

I idly fingered the centerpiece, a hand-painted accordion fan nestled in a spray of evergreens and silver balls. This one had been done by a little girl named Eliana. She had used her fingerprints to make a snowman family, white on a red fan.

All the fans had been made in my classes. A small card at the base of each centerpiece told a little bit about the kid. First name. Age. A bit of diagnosis. I wanted to go to each card and write more. Not just *Eliana, age 9, Acute Myeloid Leukemia*.

But *Eliana, with the most infectious laugh, who loves to draw ponies and use too much glitter, and wants nothing more than to go back to third grade and sit next to Jeremiah, who, according to her, is a tote dreamboat.*

Darion reached for my hand and kissed my knuckles. I smiled over at him. He was ever amazing while I brooded over life, art, and of course, Albert. My artist friend hadn't been able to talk in over a week now. It was only a matter of time. I couldn't seem to find the strength to face it yet. I pretended he would be fine again, another drug would lift him back into spirits and the ability to work.

Denial was comfortable.

Darion kissed my hand again and this time raised his eyebrows. I sat up straight. Of course. This was a signal that he wanted to get out of here. I turned to the back of my chair for the shawl I had worn over my dress.

But his plan to flee was thwarted by the hospital director walking up to the podium and looking over the tables with an eagle eye, as if daring anyone to leave. Darion sighed and settled back in his chair.

I leaned in. "Missed your op," I said.

He shrugged. "Boring motivational talks are part of the gig."

I glanced around the room. I recognized almost everyone after working here over a year. I didn't have any close friends, but I was on chatty terms with everyone. The nurses and orderlies who brought patients to my therapy room were the ones I knew the best, although precious few of them were invited to this party. It seemed to be all doctors and administrators. A few RNs. Probably charge nurses. I guessed I was the only *riffraff* who had made it in, and then only because I was engaged to Darion. I hated hospital hierarchy.

The director prattled on about patient outcomes and positive hospital culture, which sounded to me like the bad result of a Pap smear. I had to pinch my lips together to avoid laughing. But it felt good to lighten up a little. Just a little.

My phone buzzed from the tiny purse hanging on the back of my chair. I calculated the risk of looking. The room wasn't dim, so the light wouldn't show. I glanced at other tables. At least two people at each one were staring at their crotches. No doubt their phones were hiding under the table.

Fine. I could be a crotch-gazer too.

I tugged the phone out and held it under the table in my lap.

Another baby picture from Jenny. I instantly clicked the screen off. That was for later.

It had been two months since the baby arrived, and I was doing better. Somewhat. I'd actually held the little bugger on Christmas Eve. She was cute, of course, and dressed like only Jenny would do. Sparkle and color and matching shoes and headbands and blankets.

Darion draped his arm around the back of my chair. I could feel his tension, how much he wanted to leave. We all got stuck in places that made us uncomfortable, I guessed. Life marched on.

People around us clapped, and I snapped to attention. Finally, an end! A projector popped on and the lights came down as a presentation started.

"That's our cue," Darion said. "Not a minute more."

I had no desire to argue with that. I scooped up my purse and phone and shawl and followed Darion to the closest door.

When we were outside the room, I burst out laughing. "You're terrible," I said. "Skipping out on your company party just when you were learning how to create positive cultures."

Darion broke out in a broad grin. "I needed to get you home. I want to see that little black dress on the floor."

My phone buzzed again. God, Jenny and her baby pictures. Maybe it was time for me to ask her to stop. I couldn't exactly block her. Although maybe I could create a setting to automatically strip the images.

Uggh, I was doing it again. Avoiding the unavoidable.

Darion dragged me closer to him. "What's getting you?" he asked.

"Nothing. Just Jenny and her baby pictures."

"Give me that," he said, holding out his hand.

I passed him the phone. "What are you going to say?"

He clicked it on. "Just that your doctor has put you on a strict image diet of two baby pictures per day and surely she doesn't want to—"

He halted, staring down at the phone.

My heart seized up. "What is it?"

He lowered the phone and dragged me close. I knew it was bad then, real bad. He never acted like this.

"Darion, tell me," I said.

"It's Albert," he said, and at the name, my knees buckled. "He's coding."

I jerked away from Darion and took off for the elevators at a run. Darion's footsteps pounded behind me.

I punched the button, but when the doors didn't open immediately, I shot away for the stairs.

My ballet slippers tried to fall off as I hurtled up the steps two and three at a time. I pushed off the railing with every footfall, propelling myself faster.

I burst through the door and sprinted down the hall, Darion on my heels. I saw two familiar nurses outside Albert's door. When I got there, Marianna held up her hand. "You can't go in, Tina. Not right now."

Like hell I couldn't. I tried to push through, but Darion grabbed my arm. "Let them do their job," he said.

Inside, the code team surrounded Albert. I couldn't see him. Layla stood in the corner, her hands clasped by her chest.

A firm voice said, "Clear," and the unmistakable sound of paddles releasing a shock made my heart fall. I knew it would happen. But I couldn't bear it.

I turned to Darion. "How do I find out if he had an advance directive to stop this?" I couldn't imagine Albert wanting to go on, since a suicide attempt was what got him here. I wanted to kick myself for not checking on this before now.

Marianna wrapped an arm around my waist. "He had one. It was very specific," she said. "You or Layla are allowed to make the call. Layla made it."

I turned back to Layla, watching intently, her eyes red and wet.

"I need to talk to her," I said.

"The code team won't pull out once they have a directive," Marianna said.

"I know. I just want to see what happened."

She released me, and I slipped into the room, careful to slide along the back wall and out of the team's way. When I made it to Layla, she clutched my arm. "Oh, Tina, it was so scary. He choked and his heart stopped."

I wasn't going to question her decision, not right now. I knew Albert had given up his choices to make them ours. He was letting us let him go on our timetable, not his. The ultimate in trust and love.

We wrapped our arms around each other and waited to see what would happen to our beloved Albert.

A nurse shot something else into the IV. A doctor ordered a drug, something I couldn't quite understand.

The monitor on our side showed a steady rhythm.

"Move him to ICU," the doctor said. "Page Dr. Manchester."

He turned around and saw me and nodded. "We'll figure out what caused the arrest," he said. "He's stable for the moment."

"Thank you," Layla said. "When will we find out more?"

"He'll be assessed in ICU," the doctor said. "Then they should have more information about his prognosis."

Layla nodded. Two aides lifted the sides of Albert's bed and began the process of prepping him to be moved. Both Layla and I moved forward to touch his cool, unmoving arm while they worked.

We wouldn't get access to him in ICU, not without an escort. Just the depressing waiting room. My heart felt wrung out with despair. It might as well be the end.

"The last time he talked to me was several days ago," Layla said, her voice quivering. "He said, 'Take care of Tina.'" She wrapped an arm around my shoulders.

I tried to think what his last words to me had been. I hadn't known at the time we were so close to the end.

What had he said?

My eyes burned as anger flushed through me. Why couldn't I remember? It was important!

The bed moved forward, and Layla and I were forced to the side as they pushed it out the door. We followed like a funeral parade, Darion stepping alongside us once we were in the hall.

No walk had ever seemed so long or so terrible. Not the one from the hospital after I lost Peanut. Not the one up to my apartment afterward, abandoned by my boyfriend now that I wasn't pregnant and he wasn't stuck with me.

Not the one home after the doctors patched up my sliced wrists.

Nothing was like this.

At the hub of the ICU, one orderly turned back to point us to the waiting room while they headed on through to the stations. I didn't turn there, didn't look for a chair. I just watched them roll Albert away. I couldn't help but feel I would not see him again, and I had to burn this image in my mind, this last moment I might see him before he died.

When the doors slid closed behind them, Darion led me and Layla to the chairs. My legs didn't seem to know what to do, how to sit, so Darion pulled me into his lap. "Hang in there, my love," he said, cradling my head against his shoulder.

Layla probably sat somewhere, but I didn't look up. The image was seared into my mind, and I tried to hold it. I wanted to paint it, make it permanent. Paint your pain, Albert had told me so many times. Get it out of your soul and onto the page. I would paint this pain. But I did not believe it would ever leave my soul.

Hours passed. Darion did not move me, did not let me go. I held the image of Albert in my brain until my head throbbed. Finally, I asked Darion to go fetch a sketchbook from the therapy room.

All through the night I drew, madly flipping through page after page with a soft pencil, trying with earnest to get my pain on the page and out of my heart. Sometime in the early morning hours, Layla left to check on her dogs and change clothes.

I sat in my black dress, Darion next to me. I couldn't leave while she was gone. I couldn't leave at all.

The shifts would change at 8 a.m. Doctors would start their rounds. Sometime after that someone would talk to us, tell us how he was. Tests were probably run during the night. We would have answers, and an idea of what to expect.

I began to hold on to that, waiting for that moment. It eased the pain of sitting there, the ends of my fingers black from smudging the pencil sketches.

A nurse I didn't recognize came out and sat beside me. "Tina?" she said gently.

My head snapped up. I looked at her, trying to figure out what she was about to say. Nurses didn't deliver news. They took you to conference rooms where people told you things. I braced myself for her words.

"He's stirring a little," she said. "If you want to see him, this is a good time."

I jumped up, letting the sketchbook fall. "Text Layla," I told Darion.

I followed the woman through the sliding doors. I had not been in ICU much, as my patients had to have a certain level of stability to come to therapy. But I knew the rough layout. We went down the hall and passed the first ICU bay, then turned into the second.

Several beds were separated by curtains. Albert was on our end, his mass of gray curls lit up by a small light near his head.

His eyes were open.

I lunged for him and grabbed his hand. "You scared us," I said.

He nodded, just barely, but enough for me to see it. Then he tilted his head a little, as if to say, "I'm sorry."

I glanced at the setup. Tubes going into his gown. An oxygen line into his nose. Nothing too crazy. His heartbeat slid across the screen.

Maybe this was just a hiccup.

"Cat still got your tongue?" I asked. Maybe he would say something else. I would not forget it. Not ever. Now I would know how important each moment was.

He opened his mouth, but I could see he couldn't control his throat muscles. I knew this was one of the end stages of Parkinson's. He hadn't been able to eat solids for a long time, due to the choking hazard.

He enclosed my hand in his. He was struggling to stay awake now. I squeezed his fingers, a hand once so talented that the art world was at his command.

His finger slid along my palm. I thought his movements were involuntary until I recognized a letter.

I looked down. He was drawing a letter against my skin.

"*P*?" I asked him.

He gave one of the small nods.

Then an *A*.

Then *I*.

"Paint," I said with a smile. "You're still drilling that into me, right? Paint your pain?"

He shook his head for no.

"What should I paint, then?" I asked him.

The letters started up again.

H.

O.

P.

E.

Paint your hope.

12

CORABELLE

Tina and I sat in the front seat of my car long after Albert's funeral was over. I wasn't going to leave her side, not today.

Darion moved his hospital shift to attend the service, but he hadn't anticipated that Tina would refuse to leave the cemetery. So, I took over when he had to go. I could still see the black Mercedes in my rearview mirror, inching along the narrow road through the gravestones.

Everyone else was gone. The turnout had been small. Albert's girlfriend, Layla. A random uncle, clearly angling for information about the will. A couple other artists who had worked with Albert decades ago and managed to find out where the private ceremony would be.

Tina stared out the window at the semicircle of pillars that housed the ashes of those who had been cremated and stored. The flower stands were still all around, the ribbons fluttering. They wouldn't last long in this weather. A crew would come along later to attend to that, I assumed.

The chairs were scattered on the turf mat beneath a small tent. Even though the service had been brief, just a few words by a funeral home attendant, the blustery cold had been hard to manage. When we hit the hour mark after the others had left, Darion and I convinced Tina to at least sit inside the car. I knew Darion had not wanted to leave her, but it would take him a while to arrange for his shift to be covered. He assured me he would be back.

I was fine just sitting here, looking out on the peace of the rolling hills. The cemetery was beautiful and well kept. I had nowhere to be and nothing pressing to do. Emotionally, I was barely holding it together myself. Between Jenny's baby and Manuelito's mother refusing to bring Gavin's son back from Mexico, life had been difficult and strained.

Gavin was in Mexico City at the moment, trying to figure out if there was a way to force Rosa to give him visitation. When she hadn't returned after Christmas, he had gone crazy trying to find her.

Eventually we learned that her missing family had turned back up, the cousins who had raised Manuelito from birth, and she wanted to stay with them. Gavin had been shut out.

I mostly felt numb about everything. I focused on grad school, classes, grading papers.

Except now. I reached over to grasp Tina's wrist. She took a deep breath at my touch. "I'm so sorry, Tina," I said. "I thought you were doing better."

She shrugged. "I thought so too. It's been a month. Maybe delaying the service was a bad idea." She fingered the glass shell at her neck. Inside it was a small portion of Albert's ashes. The rest had gone inside the pillar for Layla to visit. She had wanted someplace to go. Tina had wanted him with her. This had been their compromise.

Albert had no descendants, since his only daughter had died when his wife drove her car into the ocean with the young girl strapped in with her. As far as we could tell, the wayward uncle was the only family, and Albert had not had any contact with him since he was a child.

"Did that uncle get mentioned in the will?" I asked. Darion had kept the man away from Tina when he pestered her. Tina was the executor of Albert's estate, and she spent the past month working with a lawyer to get everything straight and protect his copyrights.

"Yes, we're throwing him a bone," Tina said. "Ten thousand or something if he signs to stay away. The lawyer will handle it."

She hadn't talked much about the situation. She raised her hand to adjust the crocheted black cap on her head, and I let go of her wrist. She was so pale, so thin. I didn't know how she kept going. The charcoal sweater and long wispy skirt made her look tragic and lost.

I didn't know how to help her.

"We can go," she said. "I'm ready to go."

I turned the key in the ignition, wincing when the car sputtered a little to start. "It's cranky when it's cold," I said, trying to laugh. It sounded hollow.

But Tina relaxed a little. "It's a California car," she said. "It thinks you're going back on your word about the balmy winters."

We backed out of the spot and headed down the lane. She

turned her head for a moment to look at the flowers one more time, then faced front. "Well, that part's done."

"You did a great job," I said. "It was lovely."

"I kept the press away," she said. "That was the least I could do." She fingered a loose string at the hem of her sweater. "I'll tell Darion he doesn't have to take off his shift for me. I'm sorry I held him up."

"I'm happy to hang out with you," I said. "Gavin won't be back for several days."

"I can't believe he rode his motorcycle all the way to Mexico City," she said.

"It's expensive to fly, and he wanted to be able to get around in case he was able to visit Manuelito." We passed through the big open gates.

Tina took one more glance behind at the grounds.

"Will you come here?" I asked.

She faced front and gripped the glass shell again. "No. I'm not much on graveside weeping."

The streets were quiet. We were in a posh part of San Diego. Tina had spared no expense on the location. Albert had left all the decisions to her and Layla.

"Did you keep your baby's ashes too?" I asked.

Tina frowned. "No, my mother insisted on a grave." She flinched. "I think about his bones in a box in the ground, and I..." She faltered. "I can't think about it."

I winced. Finn had also been buried.

"There's no good way to do any of this," Tina said. "Picturing them in the incinerator isn't exactly comforting either."

I couldn't think about these things. "Where would you like to go?" I asked her.

Tina stared out the window. "We should stop by his studio. He left something for you, and now is as good a time as any to give it to you."

I tried to imagine what it might be. I pictured a ceramic version of Albert's famous demonic clowns and suppressed a shudder. I had admired Albert and loved his relationship with Tina. But his work? I was not a fan.

"Where is his place?" I asked.

"A couple miles up the road. I'm going to keep his studio open, do some artist-in-residence type stuff."

"Did he have a house too?"

"It's all one big estate," she said. "I still have to figure out how to handle the rest of the house, the upkeep, you know."

I didn't know much about Albert's wishes. "Is Layla going to live there?"

Tina shook her head. "No, she always had her own place. They met in the hospital, and I'm not sure she's ever even been to his estate. Between the hospital and rehab, he never was able to get out to see it again."

Her voice caught on the last word.

"You met him at just the right time for him," I said. "You brought him so much happiness this past year."

She pulled her cap off and rubbed her head. Her wispy blonde hair crackled with static. "It seemed so short."

I thought of my seven days with Finn. That had been short. But then, Tina had only three hours with her baby. We could never have had enough. How often did we ever think that time was enough? Gavin had only a year with Manuelito before Rosa took him away again.

Grandparents. Parents. Children. Pets. Never enough time. This was where we should concentrate our energy. Where we should place our happiness. But life kept going. Work. Obligations. They stole our time.

I had to stop thinking about it. My life was making me crazy. I had priorities. I wanted a family to prioritize. But I had no way to make it happen right now. I was stuck. Gavin was snipped. We were barely making ends meet. No time or money for surgery. No time or money for a baby even if he hadn't had the vasectomy.

Tina directed me through a neighborhood where each house was surrounded by fences and gates. "It's three down," she said. "The gray brick one." She dragged her brown suede knapsack up from the floor and dug around.

When we approached the drive, Tina pushed a button on what looked like a garage door opener. The iron gate glided on a track to let us through.

The road led to a circle in front of a large house with gray pillars. Everything about the property was colorless. The grass was long dead, smashed down with huge patches of dirt.

"Cheerful, isn't it?" Tina said.

"I guess it matches the personality of someone who painted demonic clowns," I said.

She sat back, surveying the house. "He was a real mess most of his career. He never got over his wife and daughter. Losing them was the ultimate failure."

I stopped the car in front of the door. "Nobody could handle that," I said. "And someone sensitive like Albert didn't stand a chance anyway."

She nodded. "The great artists are always the ones who lose it. The world is just too intense."

I killed the engine, but Tina made no move to get out of the car and go in.

"Have you been here often?" I asked.

"A few times," she said. "I got supplies for him in the hospital before his condition stopped him from working. And then…after…just once, to get the will and paperwork."

Albert was lucky to have Tina. I wondered who would be handling all this if she wasn't around. Lawyers, I guessed. People who didn't care.

She reached for the door handle and tugged on it. "Let's go. No use stalling."

I followed her up to the enormous double doors. She fumbled with a key chain.

Inside was an entryway done all in black and white. The floor was a traditional checkerboard. The walls were striped. Two giant mirrors on opposite walls reflected into each other, creating an infinity of images. If you looked at them for long, you felt disoriented, like you were in a fun house and an evil clown might jump out at any moment.

"I hate this room," Tina said. "But there are creepier ones."

I wasn't sure I wanted to see them. I forced myself to look away from the mirror as the room narrowed and funneled us into a hall out the back. This led to a large open area with a staircase going upstairs. Everything in it was red. The floor, the walls, the doors leading in three directions. Even the metal rails circling up to a landing.

On a glossy red table in the center of the room sat a lacquered

red vase with stiff, twisted sticks shooting out of it like bloodstained party decorations.

"Albert had some issues," I said.

"You don't even know the half of it," Tina said. "We all knew the kinder, gentler version of him."

I didn't want to know anything else. I could still picture him the few times I had seen him, his wild gray curls, his friendly expression. And the adoration for Tina always on his face, as if she might have somehow been his lost daughter.

"The studio is this way. It has its own exterior door, but it's been blocked for years, apparently. I'll get it opened up again so that when we start accepting artist fellows they don't have to tromp through the evil mansion."

"Probably a good idea," I said.

We took one of the hallways leading from the red room. This one had ordinary muted gold wallpaper and was a relief from the intensity of the first rooms. Framed paintings lined the walls, a completely random assortment of everything from still-life works of fruit to landscapes to classical portraits. A few abstract pieces with blocks of color were mixed in.

"This is his hall of contemporaries," Tina said. "He bought a lot of art to support people he had met or gone to school with. Some were former students. He had a lot of friends in the early days, before the bad stuff happened."

"And after?"

"He built this place and closed himself up. There are rooms for every mood, none of them happy."

"Art wasn't an escape for him, then?" We paused by a set of double doors at the end of the hall, and Tina sorted through the keys again.

"He tried to make it one, but he just couldn't get the pain out of his soul," she said. "The evil clowns came easily to him, so he just kept doing them, over and over, sort of like a child who might rock back and forth when distressed."

I thought about my old habit of holding my breath to pass out when life got too hard. Maybe it was the same thing. The stuff we did to make it through.

Tina opened the door. The studio was like nothing I'd ever seen. It was a wing off the main house, and the top was all skylight. The far wall was also all windows.

"Wow," I said.

"Yeah, a lot of light for someone who was obsessed with one dark subject. He could have painted so many amazing things."

Several easels stood around, most empty. Cabinets and drawers covered one entire wall. Parts of the room were tidy with blank canvases and clean paint palettes. The rest was chaos, with drops piled up and brushes stuck to dried spatters of paint. Discarded canvases were stacked haphazardly, some of the stacks falling over.

"I started the process of picking up, but I might hire a service in the end," Tina said. "Long way to go before we can make this a working space."

"What happened to the assistant who found him?"

"She got spooked after she realized he wasn't dead and she'd started a bad rumor. Nobody's heard from her. She abandoned her Facebook pages." Tina shrugged. "I had the locks rekeyed and the security changed."

I walked around the room, dodging jars of oils and tin cans of turpentine. I paused by a table with a half-finished sculpture of a woman. "Was this Albert's?"

"I don't think so," Tina said, coming up on it. "He really only did the clowns once he lived here. I'd guess it was the assistant's or maybe some art student who was around. A few were still coming to work here occasionally." She touched the base. "I don't want to move anything that is unidentified, though, for the estate. Albert was big. Big enough that his last incomplete works are very valuable."

She walked to a corner where a desk with a computer felt out of place, black and modern among all the easels and paints that could have come from almost any era.

I looked at the sculpture again. The woman wore a dress, and the bottom hem looked odd, like it wasn't hanging down. Like maybe it was floating. I peered at her head. There was no hair yet, just an unformed block. "You think she's underwater?" I asked Tina. I remembered my coat floating around me in the ocean from that terrible day I walked into the water.

Tina walked back over, holding an envelope. She bent to stare at the statue. "You might be right." She kneeled down to get super close. "And the way this foot is kicked out. She could be swimming."

She touched a bit of the statue, then jerked back as if she was burned. "I recognize the marks now from the one he did for me." Her face was pink from excitement. She ran over to the desk and pulled out a magazine. She turned to an image inside, a picture of Albert when he was young, with a woman.

"Do you think this face looks like her?" Tina asked.

I held the page next to the unfinished sculpture. "Look at the nose," I said. "I'd say it's very likely."

She pressed her hand against her throat. "This might have been what he was working on. What sent him over the edge."

We stared at the woman a little longer. On the table next to it was another block of wrapped clay. "He was going to add to it," I said. "There was more."

Tina set down the magazine and laid her hand on the top of the block. "I bet he was going to try to do his daughter." Her voice faded to a rasp. "He was trying to do something else. Break out of his rut. Face his demons."

She took a step back and sat on a tall stool. "I knew when the Parkinson's started getting to him, he felt this compulsion to finish the things he needed to do." She reached out to touch the block of clay again. "But with the shaking he wasn't able to do it the way he wanted. He didn't think he ever would."

Tina stood back up. "I'll call the lawyer. Ask what to do with this. It's significant." She headed to the desk again, then stopped. She picked up an envelope from where it rested on an easel and handed it to me. "This is for you."

I took it and watched her pick up a camera to snap pictures of the location of the sculpture. Then she carefully moved it to a cabinet on the wall where it was less likely to get bumped or damaged.

I turned the envelope over. On the outside was a printed label with the simple word "Corabelle."

It was not sealed. I lifted the flap and pulled out a sheet of paper folded into thirds. Inside was a legal bit about the will. Then a small bit of paper that said, in shaky handwriting, "For the babies sure to come. Undo the hurt. Albert."

I glanced up at Tina. She was watching me now, her face serious. She didn't say anything but pointed at my hands to indicate, keep looking.

Behind the note was a check.

A check for twenty thousand dollars.

13

TINA

I couldn't stop looking at the unfinished sculpture.

I had moved it out of the studio to one of Albert's private rooms a week ago, the day after Corabelle realized how important it was to the estate. It was now safely housed in a room I could hang out in without feeling squeamish. Albert's study was steely and impersonal, from the stiff navy leather sofa to the frosty gray shelves filled with clear crystal.

But at least it didn't look like a fun house or a murder scene.

The statue of the woman stood on an empty desk in front of a set of bay windows. The block of unopened clay still rested in its position at her feet. I circled it, trying to figure out where Albert began and, more importantly, where he stopped. What was the last thing he sculpted on his wife? What broke him?

I remembered with chagrin finding some sculpting tools on the floor of his studio during one of the visits before he died. I picked them up with no clue. So important. The location of them could have told me his state of mind when he stopped working. I had been foolish to put them away in their tray. No matter how much I racked my brain, I could not remember which ones they were.

The question pulsed inside me, night and day. What made Albert snap? What led such a talented man to attempt suicide in his studio in the middle of an important work?

I wanted to know the tiniest detail and hovered over the statue. Had it been the uplifted foot? Or the outstretched arm? Those were complete. Maybe her hair? It was still a block of clay, not yet formed into a swirling underwater mass.

Or perhaps as he prepared to finish the woman, his mind had turned to the wrapped block that would become his only daughter, just six years old. He would watch her die in his hands as he sculpted. He would create her image in a way he hadn't seen, couldn't have seen, in those last moments of her life.

It would be too much for anyone.

I turned my gaze away. I had to pull myself together. I knew I was off the rails, hurtling toward disaster. I'd taken a leave of absence from the hospital, claiming I needed to manage Albert's estate. But really, I couldn't focus on anything else. Albert's puzzle felt like my puzzle. It was the only thing I wanted to think about.

I forced myself out of the room and into the hall, only to spin around and go back before I had walked even ten steps away.

The afternoon light pouring in showed the dust on everything other than the desk I had cleaned before placing the sculpture there. I could fix that, tidy the room. It would give me an excuse to stay.

The dust wipes were by the door. I could pick them up. Do the job.

But I sat on the cold sofa instead, my gaze riveted on the woman. Albert had never told me about the statue. We'd reviewed the contents of the studio, and he had told me the names of his assistant and a couple students who might have works in there, so I'd always assumed this sculpture was someone else's. Only Corabelle had made the connection.

It was too late to ask him now. Last week, I tried again to locate the assistant, Carly something-or-other. After a tussle with the college campus, I had finally gotten a cell phone number. She clearly didn't want to talk to me, though, as she never called back, and I had quit trying after the third call rolled straight to her voice mail.

I wasn't mad at her. If I'd seen Albert on the floor in front of a blood-spattered canvas, I'd have probably freaked out too. I didn't blame her for posting that he was dead when he wasn't.

But maybe there was more to it. Maybe she'd stolen something or embezzled money. I'd probably uncover something later.

I didn't care about that. I wanted information. I wanted to know more. But she wasn't giving me the chance to ask.

My fingers ached and I realized I'd been clutching the sofa cushion with an iron grip. I let go. *Calm down, Tina.*

I left the room again, this time forcing myself back to the studio. I had cleaned up another section, although my heart wasn't in the effort. I wanted to preserve the way it had been, how it had looked when Albert was last there. I took endless pictures, documenting and cataloging. I knew his will called for this space being offered to young artists. I knew I could run a program myself or I could pay someone. It was all specified in the estate documents.

But I wasn't ready. This was Albert's place. Where he worked. Where he lived and almost died.

I wanted it for myself.

I'd left my bag and my phone on a stool and felt a pang of guilt at the half-dozen text messages that had come through while I brooded in the study.

Corabelle. Jenny. Darion. My important people. Checking in. Worrying. I typed something merry sounding to Jenny, let Corabelle know I was working, and told Darion I'd be home before his shift was over.

Then I circled the room again, trailing my hand along the easels, straightening small things. This always calmed me.

I sat on a stool in front of a blank canvas. I tried to imagine what would go on it. My image of me and Peanut on the cliff was still incomplete, but I no longer felt the urge to work on it.

I wanted to spatter paint on the pristine white, red and black and silver. I realized those were the colors a long-ago ex-boyfriend had always worked in and felt horror. He was the father of Peanut, who'd ditched me after the baby died. I hated that my mind was turning to that.

Each loss was every loss.

I fed people that line back in the days when I did the suicide-talk circuit. Every time something bad happened, you revisited all your bad things. This was the cycle that led you down a path to despair. Your view of life became one of those optical illusions where you could see two faces or a vase, but now you could see only the one that scared you more. It wouldn't even occur to you to try to refocus, to see anything else.

I turned away from the blank canvas. I should get out of here, carry on, hire someone to do this work. It was dragging me down, killing me.

But instead, I picked up the outrageous key ring to try again to match up locks with keys. An entire section of cabinets was still inaccessible, and it took patience and perseverance to try each key in each lock and document which was which.

This last section was too high to reach without help. I dragged a step stool over. I pushed aside the keys that had been identified and started with the ones that hadn't opened anything yet. Sixteen in all, and after several painstaking minutes, none of them fit the large wide cabinet I was going for.

Maybe one of the previous keys also opened this one. I stepped down and made circles with my shoulders, trying to work out the kinks from my position. Time was passing. I could see the light outside the window starting to fade. Just this one cabinet, and then I would go.

I sorted keys and headed up again. Probably the dang thing was empty or had nothing but dried-out oil paints. But I'd gotten this far.

The first key wouldn't go in. The second one slid in but wouldn't turn. I jiggled it carefully to be sure. Nope.

The third key was way too large. The fourth too small.

The fifth slid in again.

I dropped my arms, letting blood flow back into my hands. Still at least six of these cabinets to unlock some other day. I glanced around. Albert sure had a lot of storage in here.

I reached up and jiggled the key. Yes. I felt the lock twist and tugged the handle.

The door was open, but I couldn't really see inside. It was too high. I needed a taller ladder. I jumped down and made a note on my sketch of the cabinets that key #5 opened it.

Taller ladder. I hadn't seen one anywhere in the house. But I hadn't searched the four-car garage. The one time I popped my head in there, I spotted Albert's small Alfa Romeo and a ton of shop machine tools. Everything there seemed in order, so I hadn't explored.

But before I could leave, something moved beyond the bushes outside the wall of windows. I paused, peering out. A car was pulling up to the driveway. I couldn't see it clearly, due to the shrubbery.

I had gotten the exterior door cleared, although it wasn't easy to open, sticking unless you jerked on it. I braced my feet and clasped the handle. After a couple sharp tugs, it pulled free.

The cool evening breeze was refreshing. I always forgot how dense the air in the studio was, heavy with the smells of old paints and chemicals. I stepped out so I could see the circle drive.

It was Darion.

He stood beside his Mercedes, looking up at the front doors. He hadn't been here before. How had he gotten in the gate?

"Darion?" I said.

He turned and spotted me, giving me a broad smile. He wore jeans and a sweatshirt, so his shift was long over. I swallowed my guilt. I really had lost track of time.

He turned back to his car and removed a picnic basket. I recognized it from the place we'd gone to on an early date, when I first saw the cliff where I would paint the image of me and Peanut. My throat tightened. Darion always knew what to do.

"Figured you'd be hungry by now," he said, striding over.

"How did you get in the gate?"

"A little trick an ambulance driver told me." He held out his hand to me.

I took it. "Oh," I said. "I'm glad you're here." And I tried to be. This was Darion. I should be happy to see him. But still, I felt uneasy, like my secret life was getting exposed.

I looked back at the house. "Do you want the grim tour?"

"Maybe later." He still held the smile, but I could see the question in his eyes. The *how are you?*

"Good idea," I said, forcing a smile of my own. "It might make you lose your appetite."

He pulled me tight against him as we walked back to the studio door. He gestured to the gray brick walls by lifting the basket. "Cheerful."

"I know. Albert was not exactly a picture of mental health during the years he lived here." I let go of Darion so we could pass through the door.

He stopped once he got inside to look over the room. "Wow. This is a nice setup." He placed the basket on an empty counter and walked around, looking at easels and some of the completed paintings. He paused in front of an image of a sunflower. "That doesn't seem like Albert."

"I'm trying to identify the artist," I said. "There were some students and interns working here too."

Darion nodded. He glanced up and noticed the step stool and open cabinet, the key ring still stuck inside the lock. "Were you able to reach that?"

"I was looking for a taller ladder when you arrived," I said.

He headed for the wall. "You want me to pull down

whatever's up there?"

"Sure." I stuffed down my resistance, the need to go through Albert's things alone. This was Darion. Maybe sharing the moment with him would help.

He stepped up. He could easily reach inside. "Sort of dark," he said, "but it looks like some wrapped paintings." He turned and stuck his arm farther back. "And something bulky."

"Be careful," I said, my excitement rising. Finished works! I knew it! I just hoped they were Albert's, and not someone else's being stored.

Darion pulled down a strangely shaped parcel in brown paper. I hurried over and took it from him. The point of something sharp poked my arm as I held it.

I set it on the desk and waited for Darion to bring down the paintings. They were also carefully taped up in brown paper. He brought them over to the desk.

"This is like a treasure hunt," Darion said. "An archaeological dig, maybe."

I carefully peeled the paper away from what felt like a sculpture. Hopefully it wasn't just some old piece of equipment.

But when the glint of a twisting gold horn was revealed, I knew exactly what I had found.

Albert's unicorns.

My knees wobbled, and Darion took my elbow to steady me. "What is it?" he asked.

"Albert made these…" I couldn't go on. It was like a relic from some bygone era, a place where no one could ever go again.

Darion tugged the rest of the paper away. "It's really beautiful."

And it was. So powerful, almost alive with energy and purpose. Its eyes bored right into you, and staring into them was unsettling, as if you'd uncovered some mysterious power.

I couldn't believe this work hadn't helped his career. But it had to be the subject matter. The world wanted pain, not beauty, in art. Suffering. The human condition.

Seeing it made me despair all the more for the life Albert could have led. His daughter could be here instead of me. He could have had grandchildren, perhaps another talented hand among his descendants.

Just the thought of passing down your passion to children brought me full circle back to the pain of my loss.

"Do you want to look at the paintings?" he asked.

I nodded, unable to speak, afraid that if I started talking, I would not be able to stop. A breakdown seemed imminent. My face flushed hot, but my body felt cold. I was all chemicals, imbalanced, blasting through me, throwing me off. Despite knowing this, I couldn't help it. Despair began to creep over me like night falling.

Keep it together, I told myself. *Focus.* I watched intently as Darion unwrapped a canvas.

Yes, another unicorn, this one just as mighty and strong as the sculpture.

Then another. But this one was different. On the unicorn's back was a small girl. Her hair was riotous with curls, just like Albert's, and light brown. She held on to the unicorn's mane with one tightened fist. The other hand was upraised, a shout into the sky.

They rode through dark green woods, sunlight shafting in between the trees.

So this was her. His little girl.

Seeing her made me lose it all the more. I couldn't look at it, look at anything. Darion reached for me, extended his hand.

I backed away. I felt sick, hot and cold and hot and cold. The weight of the engagement ring on my finger was suddenly too heavy to bear. The picnic basket. His concerned expression. His need.

He would want a family.

He would want more than I could give.

It was too much. Peanut. Albert's daughter. Albert himself.

So much loss.

"Tina?" Darion asked. "Are you all right?"

I couldn't stay here. I couldn't go with Darion. I was too lost. Too far gone. I should never have gotten in a relationship. I was supposed to stick to my one-and-done. One night. One time.

Not this.

This hope.

I couldn't hold on to hope.

I had to let it go.

I had to go.

I snatched up my purse and keys and sprinted for the door.

Darion shouted my name, but I was well ahead. I dashed for my car and dove inside. Before he could get to me, I had the car in gear and jetted around the circle driveway.

I didn't know where I was going.

But I couldn't stay here.

14

JENNY

The baby was sucking like a wee vacuum cleaner when I got the frantic text from Corabelle.

Tina has taken off.

I instinctively shifted Phoenix closer to my body, a flash of fear coursing through me. Tina had always been the one of us who acted the toughest but was the softest underneath.

It was super hard to type with the baby crushed against me, so I hit the call button instead.

"What do you mean?" I asked as soon as Corabelle answered.

Corabelle's voice was frantic. "She and Darion were at Albert's studio, and she just bolted. Drove off in her car."

"When?"

"Yesterday. Darion thought she'd come back eventually, but now it's been a whole night and she won't answer calls or texts."

"I got a chipper little text from her about six yesterday," I said. "She left after that, I guess?"

"Yes, I got one too right then. Darion said he got there around seven."

"What the hell happened?" I glanced down at Phoenix, wincing at the word *hell*. Forget Mama or Dada, her first four-letter word was probably going to be a lot more colorful.

"Darion said they found some old work of Albert's, some unicorns, and she just freaked out and took off."

"Damn." I shot another doleful look at the baby. I couldn't even think without cursing. "This is Tina through and through. Does he have any idea where she is?"

"None," Corabelle said. "He sounds pretty panicked, but I can't do anything to help. Gavin just went back for surgery."

"That's today?" Gavin had scheduled his vasectomy reversal shortly after they got the money. The docs said his best chance was to do it as soon as possible, while he was young. Not to wait until they wanted to get pregnant.

"I'm stuck," Corabelle said. "He's going to be down for a little while. I don't even know where she'd go."

"Me neither." Phoenix slipped off the latch, asleep. I shifted her on my arm. "Maybe when it comes down to it, we don't really know her that well."

"I was thinking the same thing," Corabelle said. "We hang out with her. We're friends. But we don't know anything about her past. Where she'd go."

"She was doing that painting on that cliff. You think she'd go there?" I asked.

"Darion went there after he checked the hospital. No dice."

"Where else?" I shifted in the chair in preparation for putting Phoenix down. It was harder to think with her there, as if my jitters couldn't jitter with her in my arms.

"With Albert gone, I don't really know who she hangs out with," Corabelle said.

"What about that girlfriend of Albert's?"

"Layla hasn't seen her."

"Darion would know as much as us," I said. I pinched the phone between my cheek and shoulder and carried the baby to her swing. I eased her down, holding my breath that she wouldn't wake.

"I know," Corabelle said. "He's all out of ideas."

I walked swiftly away from Phoenix now that she was down. "Okay, the baby's asleep, and I can talk better," I said. "What should we do?"

"I don't have a clue," Corabelle said. Her voice was thick. "I'm sick with worry. You know what she did before."

And I did. I'd seen those scars on Tina's arms more than once.

I paced my kitchen, closing the cabinet doors Chance had left open before taking off for some meeting. I opened the refrigerator, then closed it again. The sight of food made my stomach turn. "Well, Corabelle, if it were you — where would you go?"

Silence.

I sank down into a padded chair by the little breakfast table at the end of the kitchen. My elbow in the pink robe stuck to something sticky, but I ignored it. I had no time or energy to ponder my less-than-glamorous life. We were in full-on crisis mode.

"Corabelle?"

She sighed. Her voice was more distraught than ever when she said, "She's been talking about her baby a lot. But I don't really know much about where she's from or if she'd go back home."

"No way," I said. "She hated that place. She tried talking to her parents again after her engagement, but that didn't go too well."

"Surely she'll come back eventually," Corabelle said. "Shoot, there's Gavin's doctor. Gotta run. I'll call back later."

The signal cut out.

I set my phone on the table, wincing when I saw the source of the sticky. Something spilled. I didn't have the energy to get up and clean it right now. Phoenix was getting up twice a night again. Probably a growth spurt or something.

And now Tina was missing.

I made myself stand up again, pulling the furry robe away from whatever had it caught. A bit of pink fuzz stayed behind on the table.

I shrugged the robe off. Into the wash with that. I shivered in the T-shirt with its damp spots in front and my worn yoga pants. They had been stylish at one time, but too many spit-ups and washings had made them nubby and shapeless.

I left the robe on the chair and took my phone to the sofa to lie down. Phoenix was still out cold in the swing. Maybe I could think of something to say to Tina to get her to respond.

Surely she was seeing our messages. Just not replying. Too much pain, maybe. She could definitely get into a funk.

"Hey," I typed.

Profound, Jenny. I backspaced over it.

I tried again.

We're worried about you. A little shout-out would help us out.

I stared at the words. Self-serving, really. I was already a mother trying to make people feel guilty. I erased them.

Let me know how you're doing. I care.

That was better. But I didn't hit send. I needed to get to where Tina was. Losing Albert was just too much. I understood that part.

When Chance's sister died last year, it really felt piled on. Like there was just too much tragedy getting dumped on us, you know? It can be hard to dig yourself out, but I've got a shovel. And even though it might wreck my perfect nails, I know how to use it. Just tell me where to break soil.

That was better. I hit send, then stared dolefully at my wrecked nails. I hadn't even bothered to do a home manicure in weeks. I glanced around the room.

Clothes piled up on the back of the sofa. We mostly didn't bother changing the baby in the nursery, but had a stack of diapers and a wipe warmer right here on the coffee table.

I held the phone to my chest and stared at the ceiling, the only uncluttered part of my house. It didn't matter.

Nobody came over here except my mother. I had no friends with kids, so I couldn't really hang out with anyone. A lady with a baby was a buzzkill on a red carpet. I didn't know how to meet people like me.

Meanwhile, Chance was living the life. Industry parties. Preparation for the album release. Because he'd gotten a leg up by meeting Dylan Wolf, he always had someone to see, people to talk to, events to attend.

The money was terrible. A singer starting out was all expense and no profit. I would have to go to work soon unless we could really squeeze a lot out of the last of his signing bonus. If the album did well, there would be royalties. But creative accounting might eat that, and it would be months before a check would get cut.

Down the line, things would be good. But right now was the worst. You had to look good and live the life, but you weren't paid yet. And here Chance was, getting dragged down by the wife and baby. He couldn't live lean and party hard.

My phone buzzed and I jerked it up. It might be Tina!

But it wasn't. Just my mother, saying she'd come over midafternoon.

I should be grateful. I had help. And Phoenix was alive and healthy. So much more than what Tina and Corabelle had known. I got that.

But I was saddled with this terrible need. It had been there as long as I could remember and hadn't faded by meeting Chance or getting married or with the birth of the baby.

I needed people, bright lights, flashbulbs, attention. I wanted to rub shoulders with fame, to carry their torches, cozy up to their glamour.

And now that all this had begun, I was stuck. Home. Alone. Shivering in a wet shirt in a disaster of an apartment. Smelling of sour milk and spit-up.

We were all a mess, all three of us.

But I was going to do something about it.

I got up, stripped off the clothes, and instead of dropping them where I stood, headed to the bedroom.

Time for laundry. And to do my hair. And my nails. And get

the baby out in the fresh air. And check in at my office. Make a time line for going back.

And find Tina. Help her.

We were all going to get our lives back.

Me first.

15

CORABELLE

I paced the sidewalk outside the outpatient surgical center. I couldn't stand the waiting room one more minute. The girl at the desk assured me that they would call my cell phone if I wasn't in the waiting area when Gavin got out of recovery.

The day had warmed up, so I stripped off my jacket. Birds were singing. The trees were already leafing out even though it was February. California was like that. Winter was a weekend, not a season.

I wasn't sure if I should keep trying to text Tina. Her messages had to be stacking up. Where was she? Why exactly did she run?

But I knew. It didn't matter the trigger, just that there had been one. The moment that set you off didn't have anything to do with the big things, like someone dying or losing your job or crashing your car or a big argument. It was the last little thing, the feather that tipped the scale.

I didn't get why that was true, but I knew it from experience.

My worst nights after Finn died weren't in the hospital when he took his last labored breath, or the funeral, or arriving home to an empty house.

It was coming across a blue ribbon the same color as the one from a favorite shower gift. Spotting a Baby's First Christmas ornament in a store. Somebody asking you if you had kids.

Those were the things that did you in. They snuck up and nailed you like a snakebite in the grass.

Or a plastic bag to the face.

Heat rushed through me as I pictured myself as if I was someone else, lying on the floor of my dorm room, breathing against the plastic stuck to my cheeks. That girl felt disconnected from the person I was now. Had to be. I couldn't be putting Gavin through this, trying to get his fertility back, if I wasn't well enough to handle it. No way would I fall that far again.

I sat on a metal bench on the corner of the block. Unless it failed. How would I manage that? That sort of blow?

My breathing sped up in its old familiar way. Hyperventilating. I clutched the arm of the bench. No, I was not that girl anymore. I was steady. Calm. I could handle things.

I rolled the jacket in my hands, holding tight. This was no time to fall apart. Gavin and I had made a very difficult decision about how to use the money Albert left us. We could hire a lawyer to fight Rosa over Manuelito. Or we could reverse his vasectomy.

Gavin felt sure Rosa would do the right thing in the end. That she would tell Gavin where they were in Mexico, let him see his son. And two consultations with lawyers told us what we already knew — fighting in Mexico was a whole different battleground. The money might not even be enough to get it done.

So we had called a doctor instead.

My phone buzzed. I jerked it from my pocket. Gavin was out.

I leaped from the bench and hurried back to the surgical center door. The reversal would work. It had to. It just had to.

The woman in pink scrubs waited for me by the hall door. "For Gavin?" she said.

I nodded. She gestured for me to follow. We walked past a couple closed rooms, then the hall opened into a large area sectioned with curtains. She pulled one aside.

Gavin lay back on the bed, his hand covering his eyes.

I leaned over him, ruffling his hair. "How are you feeling, tough guy?" I asked.

"Like I've been run over by a truck," he said.

The girl laughed. "He's coming out of it. I'll bring him some juice and crackers."

Gavin moved his hand, squinted in the light, then covered his eyes again. "You're going to change my ice packs for me, right?"

I glanced down at his groin. He was extra bulgy. "And here I thought you were just happy to see me."

He groaned. "Don't even talk like that. We don't want to encourage it —" He groaned again. "Maybe I should have had Mario pick me up."

This made me laugh. "Sorry. I'll try to avoid disturbing the equipment until it's fully functional."

The girl popped back in and set a package of graham crackers and a little container of orange juice on the tray by the bed. "We'll give him about ten minutes, then I'll come by with a wheelchair. He can sit up if he wants." She hurried out again.

"Slam, bam," Gavin said. "Snip, wake up, out the door."

"That's the way they do it now. Saves costs." I pressed a button on the bed to lift the top section. "Let's get you up and at 'em."

Gavin dropped his hand, reconciled to having to face the rest of the day.

I opened the top of the juice. "Some calories will help," I said. "I swear fasting is half the problem coming out of anesthesia."

He drank it down. "Is the doc not even going to stop by? Tell us how it went?"

I wondered that too. Having procedures done at these facilities was very different from a hospital. But this urologist was supposedly the best at reversing vasectomies. He had not given any guarantees, but given Gavin's age, said we could be hopeful.

The girl nudged the curtain aside with a wheelchair. "Time to fly!" she said. She turned to me. "You want to bring your car around while we discharge him?"

"The doctor isn't going to let us know how it went?" I asked.

She picked up a folder and tugged out several pages. "I have your discharge papers here. Says you will make a follow-up appointment with him and they'll do an analysis." She handed the stack to me.

I glanced at Gavin. I guessed there was no way of really knowing until he had healed.

"Thank you," I told her.

"Pull around through the circle drive," she said merrily. "We'll be there."

I headed back down the hall and out to the front. My old car waited for us. We could have used the money for that. But we hadn't. We had rolled the dice.

I unlocked the door, not that anyone would steal this old heap. Thankfully Gavin was a mechanic and could keep it running.

I couldn't think about how we would feel if it turned out that we spent Albert's legacy for nothing. If the vasectomy was not reversible.

But then, what if it worked? What if I got pregnant?

And another baby was premature. Another NICU stay.

Another baby in the ground.

I clutched at the steering wheel. How would I manage that? Where would I bury this one? Where would I put his grave? Here in California? Or back in New Mexico with Finn?

He was so far away.

I remembered talking to Tina about how there was no good way to let go of a baby. How she had held on to that necklace with Albert's ashes as if it were her only lifeline.

Then I knew.

I knew where Tina had gone.

The cemetery back home.

She had gone to get her baby.

16

TINA

The wind whipped my hair as I walked frantically along the path, desperately trying to remember which way to go.

I hadn't been here often. Three times, maybe four.

Guilt stabbed me. I crossed my arms over my belly, wishing I had something warmer to wear. But the bitter cold would keep me alert. It had been a long, hard three-day drive alone with my raging emotions, vacillating between bitterness and despair.

The trees shivered, dropping the few fragile leaves still clinging to their branches. I was back in Texas, where winter was really a perpetual fall. Houston, my home, my nemesis. I had never hated a place more.

And this cemetery was about the worst of all.

Surrounded by huge walls to keep out road noise.

Attached to some seedy pathetic little funeral home that overcharged for their shoddy services.

Poorly kept up. Depressing and dead.

I couldn't remember where they kept the babies. I knew Peanut was in some special area. My parents were too young to have a family plot already. We didn't have a lot of money, and insurance on the kid of a kid isn't a lot. We had something like two grand to work with.

Regardless, my mother wouldn't hear of her grandbaby getting cremated. I hadn't had much say in any of it because I was back in the hospital getting my wrists stitched back together. Due to that, Mom had arranged everything herself, putting together some sappy dirge-filled funeral-home grief show that I didn't want to be at myself.

Pretty much no one came. Nobody at my school for pregnant girls knew what happened. I think maybe an administrator popped in for a couple minutes. My grandparents were dead. The baby's father was already poking some other hole. Well, probably not yet. But he was on the lookout. His vacating our garage apartment was what sent me over the edge.

Nothing was good here. Nothing. I had been right to leave.

But here I was.

Leaves crunched beneath my chunky boots. I felt adrift, wandering lost among the dead.

Then I stopped. Everything aligned, like a camera lens coming into focus.

This was it.

All the graves spread out in front of me were low. Toward the back was a large angel statue.

There were more graves than I remembered, but of course, it had been five years, six, really. Many more babies to bury.

I paused, hair in my face, wishing I'd thought to bring my hat.

My eyes watered in the cold wind as I stepped between the rows, peering at names. So many of the little stones bore only a single date. Babies who left on the day they arrived.

Like mine had.

Where was he?

I spotted a bush that seemed familiar. It was cut into the shape of a ball, sitting by a bench, like an oversized beach toy nobody would ever play with. Horrible idea, but they'd kept it up all these years. If I was right, Peanut's grave was angled off from it.

I stepped carefully through the dead smashed grass, avoiding the headstones, wincing at the thought of the tiny skeletons in their small boxes below my feet. I hated that part of walking in cemeteries. You couldn't help but tromp over people's bones.

My heart beat faster as I recognized some of the names on the carved stones set into the ground. I'd read them before on walks like this years ago. The consonants and syllables had left impressions, a signature burned directly onto my memory.

I had arrived.

The stone was small and gray and printed with simple text.

Peanut Schwartz.

February 3, 2009.

Uncut grass had encroached on the corners and then died, brown and wispy, fluttering with each gust of wind. I pushed it all aside so the edges of the grave were clear. No one had been here in a long time.

"Sorry, Peanut," I said. "I just couldn't come home for a while."

I should never have let them bury him. I could still picture the tiny powder-blue coffin. I was probably sitting on it right now.

And inside it would be the baby, threadbare bits of his sleeper spread over whatever was left of him.

I couldn't bear it.

If I had a shovel, I'd take it to the ground right now. Slam the point into this cold hard earth and get my baby out. Take him to be cremated. Keep him with me.

I never should have left him.

During a pit stop yesterday in Arizona, I called the caretaker to ask how to have the grave exhumed. I was forced to leave a voice mail, and I hadn't heard back.

But I had money now. I would make this happen.

Another sharp gust of wind sent leaves dancing. This one didn't bring me down, though. A wave of exhilaration surged through me. I felt powerful and in control. I would right this wrong.

I held on to my necklace, the shell with Albert's ashes. I would mix some together. Carry them always. No one would tell me I couldn't. My life was my own. I would bear my grief however I chose.

Something crunched behind me, and I jumped to my feet, my heart thumping.

I almost fell backward in my haste to turn around. My heel caught on the grave, and I stumbled, horrified that I was stepping on Peanut's grave. I lunged away, finally finding my balance again.

That's when I saw her.

My stomach turned. I hadn't looked at that face in five years.

My mother.

She held out her hand. "I didn't mean to scare you."

I took a step back, carefully avoiding the grave.

"How did you know I was here?" I asked.

She retracted her arm and tugged her worn sweater more tightly around her middle. She looked older than I remembered, her thick hair almost completely gray. She must have stopped dyeing it.

"The man who runs the place called with a quote to get the grave exhumed," she said. She looked uncertain now. "He had my number on file. I hadn't contacted him, so I figured it must have been you."

"Have you been waiting here?"

She stared out at the sky, tucking a loose bit of hair behind her ear. The rest was tied up in a messy knot. At last she said, "I asked him to call me if anyone showed up near the baby graves." Her eyes dropped to the stones, seeming to count all the loss that surrounded us. "I knew you would come back one day."

"I called you," I said, feeling my defenses rise up. "I let you know I was getting married."

Her gaze moved back to my face then, searching my features, looking for an answer in my expression. "It was wonderful to hear that news." She glanced down at my ring. "It's lovely."

I resisted the urge to cover it with my hand. I had vowed not to shut my family out any longer. I had promised it to myself. But I hadn't done it. A phone call or two, prodded by Darion. Birthday cards, at least one to Mother. I might have forgotten Dad's.

"I had hoped you'd come for Christmas," she said.

"My friend was dying," I said. "I couldn't leave."

She nodded. "I understand."

"He did die. In January." My words were a rush. I wasn't sure who I was trying to justify my absence to — my mother or myself.

She took a step forward. "I'm so sorry. She must have been

special to you."

"He," I said before I could stop myself. "Albert. A painter. I was learning from him."

I didn't want to talk about this anymore. I was distracted from my purpose. I turned around and sat cross-legged in front of Peanut's grave. Maybe she would take the hint and go away.

But no, she sat next to me, her practical thick-soled shoes sticking out from her paisley skirt. She shivered. "Didn't predict the cold," she said.

You can go home, I thought, but didn't say it aloud. I was freezing too but wouldn't admit it.

"He was such a lovely baby boy," she said.

My eyes smarted with tears in the cold. My anger rose up, but I stuffed it down. This is what I was supposed to be doing. Grieving. Processing. Figuring it all out.

She cared about him. So did I. I had to get control of my reactions.

"He'd be what — six now?" she said. "Tearing around, getting into things. First grade."

I could sense her wistful smile even though I refused to look. I didn't want to see her version of Peanut. I only wanted my own. He was mine.

But she went on. "My first grandbaby," she said. "And when I got the news you were getting married, I couldn't help but hope there might one day be more."

"He can't be replaced," I said, my voice dark and bitter.

"Of course not," she said. "He'll always be the first."

I refused to talk, waiting out the swirling emotion. I felt my anger drain away like a swimming pool emptying out. There was a lot of it to let go, so we sat a long time, enduring the wind and the cold.

But before I could say anything else, she stood up. "Come home for a while. Let me make you some coffee. We can go over the numbers the caretaker sent me. I'd love to hear your plans for Peanut."

She held out her hand. The heat rose in me again, that old familiar resistance to her I'd known my whole life. Where did it come from? It was so persistent. So hard to stuff down.

I forced myself to take her hand and let her help me stand up.

If I was going to get better, get past my hang-ups and put my life back together, it might as well be now.

And it might as well be with my mother.

The caretaker sat across from me and Mom, grim and serious. He wore a black suit and tie. We were in his office, small but tidy. Even though this cemetery was bare and sparse, the sales office gave the impression that your family would be taken care of.

He pushed a paper across the table showing the expenses. "We need some permits," he said. "And a funeral director oversees the process of opening and closing the grave." He tapped a line. "This is for transport to the crematorium."

My mom gasped, but I didn't blink at the number. I had zero interest in cost. I just wanted my baby out of the ground. "How soon can we do it?" I asked.

"Depends on the city," he said. "It's the permit that delays it."

"What sort of permit is it?" Mom asked.

"Just a hoop or two to jump through to make sure all is in order," he said evasively.

But I already knew. "That there isn't a public health threat," I said. "And that we aren't stealing it."

The man's expression didn't change. Funeral directors should be poker players. They'd never give a thing away.

"How long to get the permit?" I asked.

"Could be a few days if the right person is in the right office and actually doing their job. Or, could be a week or more," he said.

"And what about your part of it, once we have the permit?" I asked.

"Just a day to work around any funerals," he said evenly. "We want quiet for the serenity of this work."

And to not upset anyone that I was checking out while they were checking in, I surmised.

"Will I see him?" I asked. I'd been watching grave exhuming relentlessly on YouTube. I knew the casket could be opened.

"That isn't necessary," he said. "We are lucky that you chose a metal casket at burial, or this might not even be possible. Wooden caskets decay very quickly."

I knew this too. One undertaker online said that if you put a wood casket in an unvaulted grave, there might be nothing but discolored soil within five years, particularly since Peanut was so small and premature.

"But I want to," I said. After all those videos, I knew I could handle it.

Mom reached out to cover my hand with hers. "Darling, is that a good idea? Don't you want to remember him the way he was?"

I ignored her. I had stayed at her house last night, and while she had mightily tried to create a cozy mother-daughter evening with hot tea and chick flicks, I was distracted and uneasy. Closing a gap like ours wasn't going to happen without a struggle.

"I want to be there when the grave is opened," I said. "I insist on it."

The man settled back into his high-backed leather chair. "That is fine. We will let you know when we have the permit and can schedule it. The casket will be intact for transport to the crematorium. They can determine if you should view the remains prior to cremation. They handle everything with the utmost respect."

Mom sighed. "I don't know why you have to do this," she said.

The old familiar anger rose up in me. She didn't understand me. Never had. Never tried. "I want Peanut with ME."

Mom bit her lip, leaving a mark in her red lipstick. She faked a smile at the caretaker. "Thank you. Let us know when things are ready."

I jerked a checkbook from my bag and scribbled out the amount for the entire process. I slid it across the table and stood up. "Thank you," I said. I didn't wait for him to write a receipt or escort us out. I got up and left.

The halls were silent and ghostly, light flickering from fake oil lamps on each wall. The navy and gold wallpaper peeled in the corners and the wood floors were scuffed. The light probably minimized how much of the wear and tear was visible.

Everything had its false front.

We passed two entrances to viewing rooms, and I crossed

through the foyer to the double doors.

The sun was blindingly bright although the air was still quite cold. I didn't wait for my mother but kept striding right for my car. I could hear her rapid footsteps behind me.

"Tina!" she called out.

I wasn't up for acknowledging her. I needed to calm down. Why did she have to keep insisting that I not do this? Why didn't she get it?

At the last minute, I decided to turn away from the car and go to the baby section of the cemetery. Maybe I could pull myself together there. The whole point of bringing her along on this excursion was to fix things. I was still being my angry seventeen-year-old goth self.

I headed down the path toward the angel statue. I didn't glance back, but the moving shadows let me know she was following.

I should slow down, stop, let her walk with me.

But still, my legs kept on pumping.

Two women were out among the baby graves. I slowed down when I saw them, not sure I wanted an audience.

My mom caught up, breathing hard. "Tina, are you okay?"

My steps were uncertain now. Continue on through the cemetery, or head back to the car with my mother?

I could picture Fuseli's famous painting of Odysseus, shield upraised, fighting the battle between Scylla and Charybdis as waves pounded below and monsters threatened from above. A rock and a hard place. He had nothing on choosing between my mother and strangers near my baby's grave.

I longed to paint this image on canvas. The monster inside me and water crashing against the headstones. The need to get it down tugged at me with urgency, like hunger after a long fast. Maybe I could backtrack, play nicey-nice with Mother, and find an art supply store. Set up somewhere while I waited on the permit.

I turned to initiate this new plan when something about one of the women ahead made me pause. She seemed familiar.

"Tina, are you okay?" Mom asked again.

I ignored her, walking closer to the two women. Could it be? Really?

One of the women was young and slender, in a bulky sweater and jeans. But the other wore a floral dress. She was ample, maybe more ample than the last time I saw her. But of course, it had been six years.

"Stella?" I asked tentatively. The wind caught the word, and neither woman turned. I repeated it a little more loudly. "Stella?"

This time the sound pierced the air and the woman looked behind her. Yes! It WAS Stella, the woman who had run my pregnancy loss group so many years ago. Right here!

She cocked her head, her brows together. I felt a prickle of apprehension, feeling my mother's curious stare. Stella had a lot of women come through her doors, and I had been only a teenager then.

"It's Tina," I said. "With the striped stockings." I lifted my ankle-length skirt to reveal the rainbow over-the-knee socks I had mostly stopped wearing. Today had been an exception, since I would be so close to Peanut again. I had worn them practically every day back when Stella knew me.

"Tina!" Her face brightened. She reached over to the woman and squeezed her arm. "This is one of my other mothers," she said to her. "Her baby is laid to rest here as well."

The two women moved among the graves to come closer. Stella took one of my hands between both of hers and clasped it tightly. "It is so good to see you," she said. "You are all grown up."

This made the other woman tilt her head. I realized they had just placed a vase of flowers and a half-dozen balloons at one of the graves. "Is it an anniversary?" I asked the other woman.

She nodded. "One year. Stella kindly offered to come out here with me since my husband also recently passed away."

My stomach turned over. Stella released my hand and draped her arm around the woman. "So many ways for life to be hard," she said. "So many ways."

The woman hugged Stella. "Thank you for meeting me," she said. "I'm going to go."

"Let me know how you are doing," Stella said. "Don't be a stranger."

The woman headed back toward the parking lot. Stella turned back to me. "Is this your mother? I see an amazing resemblance."

My stomach flipped again. I had never seen anything similar about us.

"I'm Marcella," Mom said. "Tina's mom."

"I knew it," Stella said. Her round face beamed beneath a halo of fluffed-up hair. She reached out to shake my mother's hand. "We never met back in the day."

"Back in the day?" Mom's face was filled with confusion. "When Tina lived here?"

"Stella ran the pregnancy loss group," I said.

"Oh," Mom said. She smiled at Stella. "That was so helpful to Tina."

Like she'd know. I felt resentment rise up again. "At least somebody helped," I said before I could stop myself.

Mom flinched as if she'd been struck.

Stella stepped close and slid her arm inside the crook of my elbow. "Those were hard times," she said, all matter-of-fact. "Let's walk to your sweet baby's grave."

Did she know where it was? I tried to recall bringing her here, but I was pretty sure I never had. We walked toward the beach-ball bush, then off toward Peanut. My mother followed at a distance.

"How do you know where it is?" I asked her.

"I don't," she said merrily. "You're leading."

I realized that yes, I was setting the direction, even though it felt as though Stella was in charge. She was good at that, acting like she was doing the pushing when really you were going where you needed to go. My belly unclenched.

"I'm here a lot," she said. "Many of my mothers end up here."

"You still run that group after all these years?" I asked.

"I do," she said. "Most women have their own babies and move on, but for me, my greatest accomplishment is all of you."

We arrived at Peanut's grave. I realized for the second time that I had brought nothing for the empty flower vase built into the stone. No matter, I was getting him out of here. He would never have to lie beneath an empty cup again.

"Are you back in Houston to stay?" Stella asked.

"I'm just here to get Peanut's remains," I said. I kneeled down by his stone. "I don't like the idea of him down here in the ground."

"Where are you taking him?" she asked, pressing her hand into the grass to balance herself as she sat beside me.

"I'm having him cremated."

She brushed some dirt off his nameplate. "That's a nice idea. Then you can have him with you."

She understood. I felt calmer. It was always good to be with someone who got what you were after.

My mother caught up to us and sat down on the other side of me. "Did she tell you her crazy idea?" she said to Stella.

And just like that, I exploded.

"Are you kidding me?" I shouted. "If you had just done what I asked, I wouldn't have to be doing this now!"

Instead of looking away, as she once would have, my mother stared me down. Her hair blew around her face, disturbing her perfect arrangement. "You said a lot of things during that time." Her voice held a note of bitterness. "I never knew what you really meant and what you just said to upset me."

I had no idea what she was talking about. I didn't remember talking to her much at all. I stayed hidden out in the garage apartment as much as possible during this period.

"We weren't exactly close," I said, forcing my voice down. I avoided looking over at Stella. No telling what she was thinking about this.

"No, we weren't," she said. "Not by then. You were a very sweet child, happy and energetic. But adolescence was hard for you. You changed completely." She leaned forward and looked at Stella. "You know how they are."

"Actually, all three of my babies died," Stella said. "Never had a teenager."

Mom sat back, looking suitably chagrined. "I'm so sorry."

"It's fine," Stella said with a wave of her hand. "I had a niece who made a total mess of her life for a while. Ended up pregnant and deserted by the father. She lived with me for a while."

"Kayleigh!" I said. She and I had been friends after her baby was born and she lived with Stella. Then I'd moved away for college, and we lost touch.

"She's had two more since then," Stella said. "They figured things out."

"I'm so glad," I said. Kayleigh getting jilted by her fiancé was something we had in common, although her baby had been just fine.

"Well, I didn't know what to do with this one," Mom said.

Stella shifted near us both. "There is only one thing to do to a child who is impossible, distant, in trouble, and pushing you away."

We both turned to her as she took one of our hands in each of hers, forming a bridge between us.

My mother sounded wary when she asked, "And what's that?"

But I knew what she would say before she said it. Stella had said it many times in our group, about wayward husbands and family members and friends and coworkers and all the people who were hurtful to us after our losses, whether intentionally or by accident.

But still, the words resonated as she said them one more time, the wind whipping her thinning hair.

"You forgive them."

17

JENNY

Chance was doing so super great.

I sat outside the radio station recording room, watching him talk to a DJ through a mike that came down from the ceiling. He had headphones on, which made him look dashing and important.

My heart surged with pride.

My phone buzzed and I glanced down. Mom had sent an image of Phoenix lying on her belly, holding her head up. Man, she was growing fast. Mom was good about sending pictures when we were apart, although I had to admit I might not be the most anxious of mothers when I was away. Mom probably took better care of her than I did.

The broadcast version of the interview was piped into the waiting area through speakers. The delay was more than I expected, a lot longer than on live TV. Everything I was hearing was stuff he had said thirty seconds ago. It was particularly noticeable when he made a broad gesture with an exclamation in the room but the words over the air were calm and measured. I felt like we were in some weird time warp.

But it was exciting.

I took a quick picture of him through the window and sent out my millionth Tweet, watching for interaction. I was a hotshot at social media already, and I was milking this moment for Chance for all it was worth. Dylan Wolf's camp had already retweeted it, as I had asked, and so it was rapidly spreading. I posted links to the unreleased demo and set up an account for amateur concert footage for people who wanted to feel like they were getting in on his discovery.

Over four hundred new followers since the broadcast began.

I suppressed a little squee. With me on his team, we should give him the best possible launch for his upcoming album. I cared a whole lot more about his career than some overworked publicity specialist at the record label.

A couple young twentysomethings, probably college interns, based on their backpacks and animated conversation, came in and crossed in front of me. They had to be buzzed into the back room, so they weren't regular employees. They brought with them the smell of the wet chilly outdoors, plus something else. Something light and easy. Inexpensive shampoo and strawberry lip gloss. Trappings of youth.

I envied them for just a second, then reeled it back in. I was in the position to be envied. Married to an up-and-coming musician, a new mother, watching my man be interviewed on the radio. So much ahead of us. This was just the start.

The show went into commercial. A woman entered the back of the sound studio. The DJ waved her into a seat. He had his headset cocked off one ear.

My anxiety prickled. This woman was gorgeous. Tall, stacked, skinny, dressed in skintight glossy black pants and a shimmery top that showed tons of cleavage.

I pressed my hands against my boobs self-consciously, aware of their uneven shape since Phoenix had been favoring one over the other. If I tried pressing them together enough for cleavage like that, I'd be a milk fountain.

The woman reached to shake Chance's hand, then leaned in to kiss his cheek. My face flamed. Who was this person?

She sat down and everybody put their headsets back on. The DJ pointed at the sound engineer in the corner, and their conversation resumed. The broadcast was still in commercial, but quickly, the station's call letters came back and the jingle for the show returned.

I had a hard time listening to their past conversation while winnowing out what was happening in real time due to the delay. The woman could not keep her hands to herself, reaching over to touch Chance every time she spoke or laughed.

I wanted to rake my fingernails down the glass.

Chance pointed out the window at me and the woman turned. I gave a little friendly wave, but my eyes bored into her. She got it. Her fake smile froze. Whatever her angle was, it wouldn't happen today.

Thank God I had come. No telling what this chick would be up to if I wasn't here.

We weren't far from home, just a quick flight to Portland. At first we weren't sure we could scrape together enough money to get me a plane ticket too, but then Mom had chipped in. So, here we were, on a short two-night getaway. Chance was paid for, and so was our hotel room, so we could kick back a little.

My phone buzzed with an update. Another twenty followers for Chance.

Finally, the broadcast caught up, and the DJ introduced the woman as Amity Garrett, a music producer at some record company local to Portland. Apparently she was here to give Chance career advice as he got started.

"I hear you got a little press coverage while you were hitchhiking across the country," Amity said. "In LA?"

"I did," Chance said, his voice deep and smooth. "I met one heck of a woman my first night in Cali."

My interest perked up. He was going the sweet southern charmer route.

"As I recall, it even made the television tabloids," the DJ said.

"Yeah, that was something," Chance said. "Not my favorite brush with fame. But I might have to get used to it."

"But you got a wife out of it, didn't you?" the DJ asked.

"I sure did," Chance said. "She's here today."

I guessed that was the point when Amity had turned to me.

I glanced up at him again, but of course they were already on some other topic in real life. Chance seemed to be concentrating and serious.

"But you're a family man now, I hear," the DJ said. "Congratulations on the birth of your daughter."

"Thanks," Chance said. "It's been a whole 'nother experience, going from alone on the road to a home."

They went on to talk about some of Chance's songs and Amity gave him demographic information about his potential audience. In the sound booth, she had stopped reaching for him constantly.

I relaxed a little. Everything seemed back on track.

I scrolled through my contacts and paused on Tina. A week had passed with no word to anybody. I took a moment to send my daily message to her, something light and chipper.

Then I thought to check on a website she had asked me to set up for Albert's art fellowship program. She wanted to get the basics up for when they started accepting applications, and I had agreed to help her.

Only a few people were finding the page, but we hadn't done anything major to attract web traffic. I didn't care about that at the moment. I logged in as admin. I had a hunch about something.

And sure enough, when the back-end page loaded, I saw it.

Last user log-in, yesterday at 11:56 p.m.

I hadn't logged in last night. That meant Tina had.

She was okay.

I highlighted the IP address of the log-in and popped it into a search box. This would tell me where she was. It came up instantly.

Houston, Texas.

I had her.

18

CORABELLE

I held the ice pack uncertainly over Gavin's crotch. "You sure this is going to help?" I asked.

He peeked out from under his arm, which was crossed over his face. "At least until the drugs kick in."

I laid the sleeve of chilled gel on his boxers.

He sucked in a quick breath, then relaxed back onto the sofa cushions. "Yeah, that's better."

I sat on the floor next to him. He'd gone back to work today at the garage, a week earlier than he was supposed to after his surgery. And he'd thrown tires, when he should have waited several weeks for hard labor.

"We have enough money left over to make it for a while without you working," I said. God, I was worried sick over him doing this. What if he wrecked his recovery and all this was for nothing?

"It's Bud," he said. "He's short people and his son is sick."

"Can't Mario do more shifts?"

"He's already there. We're all pitching in."

I laid my head on his thigh. "Why did you throw tires? You got promoted from that a year ago."

"It needed doing. And I've been cooped up for a week. I wanted to do something hard."

And look where it got him. But I didn't say a word. This was marriage. He would make his choices, and I would make mine. You could save people only as far as they were willing to be saved.

"Come here," he said, and lifted me up to lie next to him on the sofa. I squeezed between his hard body and the back cushion and rested my head on his shoulder.

"I'll be all right," he said. "I'm just a little sore. Doc said I would be for a while."

I nodded against his neck. I honestly didn't know if I wanted the reversal to work or not. I wanted to try to restore his ability to have children, certainly. I wanted to reach for that possibility.

But if I didn't have to face the results, never had to be pregnant, to go through all that fear again, that might be okay. The uncertain future was easier to manage when the power to change it was no longer in our hands. We'd done our part.

"Nothing new from the private investigator today?" I asked. We'd discovered hiring someone to find Rosa and Gavin's son was a lot cheaper than bringing on a lawyer to work the courts.

Gavin shook his head. "We know where she is, but it's a privately guarded compound nobody can get into. They tried to deliver flowers or something. But Mexico, it's not like here."

"I'm sure there are places here that no one wants to send a pizza to," I said.

"True," he said. "I don't know. It's just so wild. How people can hole up somewhere and become invisible. I can't even talk to anyone there."

He fell silent, and I knew he was thinking about his goal to learn Spanish and talk to his son in both languages. But he hadn't done it. Manuelito picked up English so quickly, it hadn't been necessary, although Gavin would stew when Rosa would talk to family in Spanish just to leave him out.

"Too bad things didn't work out with her and Mario," I said.

"They were never going to be a couple," Gavin said. "Mario is still a bachelor to the core. He can barely handle himself."

"Still, if she'd settled here, things would have been different."

Rosa wasn't a U.S. citizen and couldn't stay unless she married. But the relationship between her and Gavin's friend had blazed hot and burned up fast.

"I worry about Manuel," Gavin said, his voice catching. "What he thinks about being away so long. If he misses us."

I closed my eyes, a tear escaping onto his shirt. I had been so against the little boy being with us at first, hard evidence of what some other woman got with Gavin that I might never have. But the boy himself was like a miracle, tender and kind. He was the best of all of us.

"Maybe we should have used the money to fight after all," I said.

Gavin squeezed me. "We went over this so many times. Fifteen-grand retainer just to get started. And where would we be later? All the money to lawyers and nothing done. I was there. I saw it for myself. At least the investigator found her. That's something."

The light outside was fading, but the days were lengthening.

Winter would give way to spring soon. And Manuelito had been gone four months, the whole lifetime of Jenny's baby, Phoenix.

That reminded me. "Jenny figured out where Tina is," I told Gavin.

He lifted his head. "Really?"

"Houston. I remembered when Jenny said it that Tina was from there. But she never talks about it."

"Did Jenny talk to her?"

"Not yet. She saw Tina log in to that site Jenny worked on for the artist project. I think she's going to text her at some point and threaten to go there."

"With the baby?"

I relaxed back against Gavin's chest. "I'm not sure."

Surely Jenny couldn't go. Not with Phoenix. I still had a little money from Albert, even after the surgery and the investigator fees. I should be the one. It would be the best use of it, to help out Tina.

"It should be me," I said. "It should be anyway. I'm the one who understands. The last thing Tina needs is a baby in her face."

Gavin shifted, making a small grunting sound of pain.

"Except," I said, realizing what I was missing, "I need to take care of you."

"Don't be ridiculous," he said. "I'm perfectly capable of microwaving my own 99-cent pizza."

I had to laugh. It was true that we'd been eating pretty badly with him laid up and me stressed out.

"It's almost spring break," I said. "I have a week off."

"So, go," Gavin said. "Mario and I can be bachelors."

I knocked my head against his collarbone. "I remember those days. Fistfights in bars?" I couldn't bring myself to say, "And prostitutes."

He laughed. "I might have had a little more clouded judgment then."

"I'll say."

"How about if I just lie here among my pizza boxes and pine for you?" He kissed the top of my head. "You could use a little getaway, anyway. No books or papers to grade. Just pack a few things and go."

I stared across the room at the images of Finn, and me and Gavin, and Manuelito. Tina was like family to me now. Yes, I would go fetch her.

Someone had to bring her home.

19

TINA

It didn't matter that people knew where I was now. I wasn't going anywhere.

Both Jenny and Corabelle had been relentlessly messaging me the past couple days. Jenny had somehow figured out I was in Houston. Corabelle had already booked a flight here. Not that I had told her where my mother lived. She wouldn't know where to go if I wanted to blow her off. Houston wasn't exactly small.

The tenor of Darion's messages had also changed. He asked if I had gone home, but I hadn't told him. I did occasionally respond to his messages, though, so he wouldn't worry. Or come after me. I had asked for space. Darion was good like that, willing to give it.

Not so much the girls. They seemed to need a resolution to this, now.

But I wasn't running from them. Or Darion. I was waiting. I needed to get this done for Peanut, but the permit hadn't come through yet. My mother was driving me crazy.

Stella had helped. She told me that just down the road from her jewelry shop, an elderly lady had set up an artist studio. She rented out space for people to paint or sculpt or do whatever it was they wanted to do.

The place had been a small nursery for exotic plants, so there was a small front building with an office, kitchen, and bathrooms. Then a fair amount of land with a couple still-functional waterfalls where plants had been displayed, and two greenhouses. She'd outfitted the greenhouses with easels and space heaters. The light was incredible.

Rent was super cheap. I'd paid for a whole month in advance. I could arrive as early as I wanted, as the woman had given me a key to my greenhouse. I generally stayed all day. Stella often stopped by at lunch. I didn't mind her company. Anybody but Mother.

I sat back on my stool, massaging my back. I should probably set up something more ergonomic since I was putting in so many hours. But then, the pain was comforting. It was something to feel.

The canvas was glossy with wet underpaint. I was working on an image of the cemetery where Peanut waited for me to rescue him. The angel statue, the ball shrubbery, and the flat graves were all present. The bottom of the image was photo-realistic, each dead blade of grass represented as stark and clear.

But as the image rose, it became softer and indistinct, losing its sharp edges.

I knew I wanted to paint Peanut in that haze, but I wasn't sure as what. In my drawing pads, I had sketched him as everything from a baby to a boy to a ghost, but nothing felt right yet.

It would come.

Sometimes I sat in the clear sunlight, the warmth of the space heater wafting up from my feet, and tried to feel Albert's presence. All good artists' journeys involved a spirit guide, and I knew he must be mine. I'd never had one before, other than Stella, whose plain talk and no-nonsense advice was very real and raw. It got me through. But Albert made me soar.

I let my gaze drift over the painting, unfocused, like I was under its spell. Albert told me that the image would tell me what it wanted to be, if I would just listen. This could not be rushed. The mistake was to force my hand to do the work that wasn't yet ready to be formed.

I turned to a rustling sound. Outside the greenhouse, Sarah, the woman who ran the studio, walked among the rocks. Her form was fuzzy through the glass, but I knew her gaunt figure and the wide-brimmed straw hat she always wore, even in the cold.

I fiddled with the oils, arranging them on a tray. I was annoyed at the break in my concentration, but I had to trust the image would come. Maybe I would sketch some more, keep my mind open.

The door creaked open behind me. One other painter sometimes occupied the space, but when I turned, it wasn't him. It was Stella.

"Thought I'd pop by and see if you were up for some vittles," she said. She wore a bright yellow dress that made me want to squint. There had to be something about old ladies and summer wear in the winter. Not that Stella was really old. Fifties. But she dressed old.

"Sure," I said. I was stuck anyway. I closed up my box of paints and pushed it under my stool.

"You keep your little corner nice and tidy," she said. "This person, not so much." She pointed at my greenhouse mate's easel.

Paint oozed from open squeeze tubes and murky water filled several clear glass jars. A haphazard stack of canvases covered the floor.

"He's in the middle of some grand inspiration."

She paused in front of the canvas, two gray blocks spattered with red and pink globs that slid down the surface. They had pooled in the tray below.

"Sure," she said. "It looks pretty inspired."

I shrugged. For all I knew, the guy was some huge name. I hadn't asked. The art world was mysterious. I could only comment on my own work.

"I was thinking of the little Thai place up the block," Stella said, "if that works for you. Dane hates Thai, so I go when I can."

I picked up the canvas sack I used as a purse and shrugged. Eating hadn't appealed to me in a long time. "Sounds fine," I said.

"Good." Stella put her arm around my shoulders and squeezed. "I have enjoyed getting to spend time with you this week."

"Just don't ask me to go to your meeting," I said. "I know it's tonight."

Stella opened the door. "I wouldn't dream of it. Although, you were on that talk circuit. I could use someone like you as a guest speaker!"

We circled the front building to the sidewalk.

"I think those days are behind me," I said. "I'm trying to look forward, not back."

She fell in step beside me as we navigated the cracked cement of this forlorn part of town. "That's a good policy," she said. "I endorse it wholeheartedly."

We passed her little shop. A sign on the door had a cardboard clock showing when she'd be back. "Do you actually make money on your store?" I asked.

"It pays for itself," she said. "I do better with my online shop, but I want somewhere to go. Makes me feel like I'm actually doing something."

That made sense to me. I felt I had little purpose at the moment. Adrift. Of course, I'd left my job behind. Sometimes I felt a twinge of regret for the patients who had been doing therapy with me, but if I were honest, I knew that all I was doing was getting them through a rough hospital stay. The faces switched out constantly.

I was just a blip in their lives, a job to be taken over by real therapists once they were home.

"You're deep in thought," Stella said. We had arrived at the Thai restaurant and she held open the door.

"Sorry." I went inside. The interior was dark and lit with wall lamps. The front windows were blacked out with heavy red drapes.

"For two?" a young girl asked, holding menus.

"Yes, thank you," Stella said.

We walked past a smattering of customers. She sat us near the kitchen door, which was warm and smelled of sweet sauces and bean curd.

I slid into a booth and glanced at the menu. Nothing appealed to me, but maybe some soup would be good.

"So, did you get back to your friends?" Stella asked.

"They're not exactly giving me the space I asked for," I told her.

"Did you tell them you were cremating the baby?"

I closed my menu. "I'm not up for explaining myself right now."

The girl came back with water, and we gave her our order. I was starting to feel overwarm near the kitchen door, and held the cool glass with both hands.

"So, who is in your group now?" I asked. If I could get Stella talking, she would hold up both ends of the conversation.

"We're big right now, ten or so," Stella said. "It goes up and down. I used to think it was seasonal or phases of the moon. Then I realized it had more to do with when the nurses remembered to hand out the fliers."

I nodded absently. My face was flaming. I regretted my sweater and the tights and the knit layers. I was perpetually cold, so the hot feeling was new. Maybe I was sick. Great. Just what I needed.

"Tina, are you okay?" Stella leaned forward on the table. "You look a little flushed."

A waitress passed with a tray of steaming plates. The sickening-sweet smell of peanut sauce hit me like a wave.

God, I was going to throw up.

I pressed my cool glass to my forehead. "I think I need some air," I said.

"Let's walk outside a second," she said.

I stood up. "No, no, let me splash some water on my face. You wait on the food."

Stella's face was tight with concern as I threaded my way through the tables to the bathroom. Moving away from the heat and the smells definitely helped. I went inside the dank little room and stared at myself in the oval mirror. My face was washed out. I didn't feel hot anymore, but clammy.

Nooo, I could not get sick right now. My mother would be even worse than she already was, doting on me. I wouldn't get a moment's peace.

I turned on the water and let it flow over my fingers. But this brought on a chill, making my stomach quake. I was going to have to go home at this rate. Damn it.

I pulled a wad of paper towels out of the dispenser and dried my hands. I'd have to bug out on Stella.

The smells assaulted me when I went back out into the restaurant. I could identify everything I passed. Pad Thai. Green curry. Lemongrass.

Stella was ahead of the game, dumping our orders into takeout containers. She saw me and waved me to the front door. I gratefully obeyed, pushing through and leaning against the crumbling bricks of the outside wall.

The day was bright and cold. The crisp air made me feel one hundred percent better. It cleared up so fast and so completely that I felt silly for having abandoned the meal. Maybe it was just something strong smelling that got to me. Maybe incense or somebody's perfume. That had happened to me before.

I turned to head back in, but right then, Stella came out, holding the bag of containers. "Tina!" she exclaimed. "Poor lamb. Are you all right?"

"I'm fine," I said. "Something in there just got to me."

She tilted her head, assessing me. "Fine?"

"Absolutely." I gave her a bright smile. "We can eat this in the greenhouse, I bet. Or at your shop. You have a back room, right?" I started walking that direction.

She fell in step beside me. Her lips were twisted to one side, like she was thinking. "Have you talked to Darion?"

That was out of the blue. "Sure," I said. "I text him once or twice a day. He's been willing to give me some time to figure things out."

She nodded. "How do you think he'll take the news?"

I had no clue what she was getting at. "What news? That I'm having Peanut cremated? I don't think it matters to him."

She stopped walking. I halted too and turned around. "Stella, what is it?"

"Are you trying to hide it from me or do you just not know?" she asked.

I was getting annoyed. "What are you talking about?"

Her kind eyes stayed on me. "Tina, maybe it's just obvious to me because I've seen so many mothers who have suffered a loss avoid acknowledging their condition until they are able to handle it. But it is clear as day."

She stepped closer and shifted her purse and the food bag to one hand so she could use the other to close around my fingers.

I had a feeling I knew what she was about to say. The awareness of it had been just under the surface. I had purposefully turned it aside, pretended it wasn't true. But her words were going to confirm it.

Her face was kind, as if she knew everything I was thinking. "It's all right to be afraid, Tina. But you will have to face it. You're pregnant."

20

CORABELLE

A lady with a toddler stood six inches from me, her baby boy on her shoulder. He had sandy blond hair and big blue eyes. His mouth right now was a huge toothy smile, unlike for most of the flight, where he wailed his heart out.

Now that we were on the ground and standing to get off the plane, he had decided to be adorable. I squashed my anxiety about what I would have to do to find Tina and tried to enjoy the moment, the cute little thing now making crazy faces at me. I wondered what Finn would have been like at his age, and my heart staggered again.

Focus on your mission, Corabelle.

We moved forward finally, and I struggled to keep from banging the man behind me with my overstuffed duffel bag. I had traveled as light as I could and checked nothing, unsure of where I'd be going or how I would be getting there.

The only thing I knew for sure was that the school for

pregnant teens Tina had attended, one of my few clues, had closed years ago. But the principal back then was Emmalou Banks, and she was now the principal at a private high school. I had the address, and I could either spring for a taxi or attempt to follow the labyrinthine bus schedule to get me there.

Probably I would take a bus partway, then hop in a taxi when it would be half the cost. Otherwise, I risked not making it before school let out. It would be close anyway, since it was already after noon.

We arrived at the front of the plane and the pilot waved as we passed. He gave the toddler a high five. Once free of the tight confines, I moved quickly. I could only hope the principal was there today. Thankfully my California college spring break had not aligned with the week off students got in Texas, or this would never have worked. I would have had to follow some other clue.

Searching for Tina's parents hadn't worked. I didn't know their first names and Schwartz was pretty common. Tina wasn't big on social media, and even studying her few Facebook friends yielded no family members or even friends from the Houston area. Her past was a blank.

But I did have the pregnancy loss group too. The woman in charge was named Stella, and I had left her a message. I was almost positive I'd heard her name before, so this had to be the one. If the principal didn't pan out for at least a parent name, I would try her again in hopes that Tina might have contacted her since she was back. Or might have records from back then where Tina's parents lived.

I'd never been on a goose chase quite this wild.

Of course, now that I was here, maybe Tina would relent and

meet me. She had responded with a simple "What!" when I told her I had bought a plane ticket to Houston.

The airport was bustling with travelers. I followed the signs to the ground transportation. If I didn't see the bus I needed within fifteen minutes, then I'd just hop in a taxi. I wasn't broke or anything, not after Albert's gift, but the frugal college student in me wouldn't let me waste money when it wasn't necessary.

The doors slid open to the bright, chilly afternoon. The sidewalk was crazy with people, suitcases, taxis, and shuttles.

I struggled with my duffel and my purse, trying to find the piece of paper where I'd written the number of the bus that got me within taxi distance of the high school. People flowed around me, already knowing where they were going and heading to their destinations.

The duffel slipped off my shoulder. I bent over, trying to catch it, groaning as my purse tipped and dumped the contents. I kneeled on the sidewalk, capturing a rolling tube of Chap Stick and a pen. Honestly, I wanted to sit on my butt and cry. What crazy idea had this been? I missed Gavin already. I wanted my apartment and my books and my schedule.

"Normally you think all this through," a voice said.

I looked up.

It was Tina.

She bent down and collected my things. "Purses that zip are a lot more practical for travel," she said.

I wanted to hug her. "You're here!"

"Yeah. Gavin sent me your flight information. I never say no to a hot guy." She stood up and handed me the purse, all put together again.

"Thank you for coming. I didn't exactly honor your request for space." Now that she was here, I felt a twinge of guilt for invading her getaway. She didn't seem to be dying or falling apart.

"You guys worry too much," she said. "Come on, I'm parked in the garage."

I hefted my bag on my shoulder. Tina wore a dark gray sweater with a short black skirt. Her legs were vivid in red and black tights. Her hair was in pigtails. She was as pale and thin as she'd been when she left, but something about her seemed stronger, more determined. Being away had been a good thing, it seemed.

The dim parking structure was colder than outside, and I shivered. We passed a couple rows of cars, then Tina hit the button for her silver Jeep. She opened the back for me to toss in my duffel.

When we settled in the front and she was backing out of the spot, I asked, "So, where are we going?"

"I have an appointment this afternoon," she said. "A grim one. You probably want to hang out at my parents' house or something."

"What are you doing?" I asked.

We exited the garage back into the sunshine. Tina's hair was flaxen in the light. As she turned the wheel, I realized she'd painted her fingernails black. Very unlike her.

"Today's the day I spring Peanut from his hellhole," she said. "They open the grave, pull out the casket, then we ride with it over to a crematorium."

My throat constricted. Despite all this, she had come to pick me up.

"Would you like me to be there?" I asked.

She shrugged. "My mother has insisted on coming along. So is my friend Stella."

"The pregnancy loss group leader."

She glanced over at me. "Yes. You did some homework."

"I was ready to try to find you."

We pulled up to the exit plaza, and she handed a couple dollars to an attendant.

Tina drove out of the airport. I waited until we were back in the flow of normal traffic before I said, "I'd like to be there, if that's okay with you."

She nodded. "I figured when you were arriving in time that fate was getting you here. Just wanted you to know what you were in for."

"I'll be fine."

Tina looked over at me. "Not every day you dig up a grave."

"You didn't want Darion here?"

At that, she pinched her lips together.

"I'm sorry," I said quickly. "I can stay out of that." But inside I felt a thrum of panic that maybe they were splitting up. How could we not have known that? They seemed fine.

But couples often did.

"This is separate from him," Tina said. "It's my thing."

I couldn't imagine doing anything this emotionally traumatic without Gavin, but then, he had been my baby's father. Tina had gone through all this alone the first time. Maybe that was how she had to do this too.

"If you're hungry or anything, tell me now," Tina said. "We can stop on the way. After this process starts, though, I think we're in it for the day. Although I guess we could have the hearse stop at McD's."

I smiled. She still had her wry humor. "It might be interesting to see how many unexpected things we can do in 24 hours."

"Challenge accepted," Tina said, but her face was still tight. "I get the impression Stella was a wild child, so she'll be on board. As for Mother, well, traumatizing her is apparently something I do well."

We got on an expressway and continued in silence. I tried to imagine what it would be like to dig up a grave. This certainly wasn't what I'd expected to happen within the first few hours of arriving.

"I should tell Gavin I made it," I said, pulling out my phone.

"Don't let on what we're doing just yet," Tina said. "I'll tell Darion in my own time. The guys might talk."

"Of course." I couldn't imagine Gavin calling up Darion to gossip, but I would keep this to myself. I texted a quick note to say Tina had met me at the airport and not to worry. Then I sat back to look out at the city.

Houston was industrial and gray. We drove up high on the expressway. Below were endless buildings and strip malls. I could see downtown in the distance, the skyscrapers stark and cold against the white sky.

Tina had not liked it here, this I knew. We drove and drove, only the signs changing. The view was remarkably similar no matter how much time passed. It reminded me of LA. Perhaps all big cities seemed the same from above. Only when you got down at the people level could you see the beauty and uniqueness of it.

We exited finally and took a huge four-lane street across town. There were trees at least, and some green here and there. Then I spotted a cemetery and figured this was it. Sure enough, Tina turned into the gate and we parked in front of a large building.

A woman in a black dress got out of her car when we opened our doors. She came up to Tina and gave her a huge hug. I assumed this was her mother.

"My lamb," she said. "Are you ready for this?"

Tina pulled away. "As ready as I can be." She turned to me. "This is my friend Corabelle. She flew in from San Diego. Corabelle, this is Stella."

I hid my surprise. "Nice to meet you. You run the loss group, right?"

Stella nodded. "I do." She reached for my hand and clasped it. "You're the one whose baby lived a few days, yes?"

I swallowed the sudden lump in my throat. So, Tina had mentioned me. "Yes, Finn lived for seven days."

"Sweet little love. What a beautiful baby he must have been," Stella said. I could see why people turned to her. She said only the comforting things. No platitudes or I'm sorry. Just affection and concern.

"He was," I said.

Another car door closed, and we turned to another woman, gray-haired and clearly Tina's mother. They carried themselves the same. She also wore all black, including a funny little pillbox hat that made her seem from another era.

"This is my mother, Marcella," Tina said. "Mom, this is Corabelle, from San Diego. A friend of mine."

"So good of you to come," Marcella said. "It's important for Tina to have friends here on a day like today."

Tina turned toward the door of the funeral home. "I guess this is it," she said. "We're a little late due to my side trip to the airport, but it'll be all right."

I felt another twinge of guilt.

"Close enough," Stella said.

We headed into the building, four serious women set on a very hard task. I wished I wasn't in jeans. Sometimes in life you had to meet a situation as you were. And I was glad I could be here for Tina.

21

TINA

The caretaker led us out to the baby graves. Another woman in a black suit followed our little group out.

I was tempted to ask the man about the beach-ball shrub, but recognized that this was just my mind trying to avoid the hard stuff in front of me. So, I didn't.

The air was completely still, as if the world itself was holding its breath. A couple men in overalls were out among the headstones, waiting. As we grew closer, I could see they had covered the surrounding graves with green Astroturf carpets. A little mound of dirt protected by a tarp sat nearby.

The videos I'd watched didn't really apply to this situation, as far as I could tell. There were always huge cranes that had to lift the casket out. But Peanut's was so tiny. As we got closer, I could see the depth of the hole. Babies weren't buried six feet down like adults, at least not here. As we approached the perfectly cut rectangle of dirt, I remembered now that my father and a friend of his had lowered the casket down.

My footsteps slowed, and even though I was behind him, the caretaker also dropped his pace. Sixth sense, I guessed. My mother clutched my hand. Stella and Corabelle walked next to us.

Despite my reluctance, we still arrived. We were quite close to the open grave before I could see the top of the bluish metal casket. It was slightly discolored, but the men had cleaned the top, so it gleamed in the sun.

I could picture myself, the last time I saw it, my arms screaming from the stitches in my wrists because I refused to take any pain medicine. I had wanted to feel it all, each line up my arm. My greatest fear then was to be numb to everything.

There was this huge black void then, and it loomed all around me. I was petrified of falling in.

Albert had taught me I was supposed to dance around the edges, laugh in its face. I still was afraid. *I'll try harder*, I promised.

The caretaker motioned to the men. They both kneeled down and grasped the handles on either side of the casket.

Bits of mud dropped off the bottom as they lifted it and laid it on the green carpet next to the grave. The headstone had also been removed, resting on another carpet a few feet away.

As we had previously agreed, the men picked up the small headstone and laid it in the empty grave. It would be filled in and left. I hadn't told my mother this, so she let out a little cry as she realized they meant to leave it there. But she did not protest. I couldn't imagine what else to do with it.

My father was away on business, and I had asked Mother not to tell him, as he would have disrupted his work to come. Having the four women there made it feel more sacred, the way tombs were once cared for in antiquity. The power of what we were doing felt timeless.

The male and female caretakers moved forward to lift the box. They were supposed to carry it to the hearse waiting on the narrow road that wound through the cemetery. But when they bent to reach for it, Stella said, "I wouldn't mind taking one of those handles, if it's okay with Tina."

I nodded. As she walked over, Corabelle followed her and took the other side. And so, it turned out that the two women who knew best where I had been, my old friend and my new, carried my baby across the lawn to the black car that waited.

My mother and I followed. This was the easy part.

The caretaker held open the back door for me in the town car that would follow the hearse. The crematorium was a few miles away. Mother slid in next to me, and after a moment, Stella sat in the front and Corabelle joined us in the back.

No one spoke. Mother pulled a handkerchief from her purse and handed it to me. I spread it out on my lap. Along one corner, in pale blue letters, she had embroidered the word *Peanut*. The outline of an angel blowing a horn was below it in gold.

"Thank you," I said. I had precious few keepsakes for the baby, just the blanket he had been wrapped in and a hospital bracelet. Each thing was something to hold on to. I found that I wanted to remember things now. I wanted to feel them again. My scars were healed over, but the wounds in my heart were open wide.

I longed, stupidly, ridiculously, to see the baby's father, jerk that he was. At least he was connected to all this, even if only by DNA. At one point, he had been interested in the baby. But now, my life had moved far from here.

Suddenly I was so grateful for my mother. She had been there. She had seen him. She knew what he looked like, how heavy he felt to hold.

A picture. I should have brought a picture.

My stomach heaved and a sob escaped me. It seemed silly now, just riding in the car, to start getting emotional. But it happened anyway. Mother took my arm and held it tight. I hadn't intended to actually use the handkerchief, but now I pressed it to my eyes.

My mother had known.

Corabelle leaned over and rested her head on my shoulder. I was surrounded with love and support. So different from the first time, when I felt utterly alone. I had refused to let anybody in.

We pulled up to another funeral home and stopped beneath the canopy by a side entrance. This place was vast, with wings stretching out on either side.

A funeral director in a somber suit came out and shook hands with the ones from the other home. Two more men in suits rolled out a small velvet-covered trolley and headed out of our view. The woman opened our door.

"This way," she said.

By the time we all got out of the car, Peanut's casket was waiting atop the trolley. When we were all assembled, the two men rolled it into the building and the director gestured for us to follow.

They had cleaned the casket during the journey. It caught the lights as it moved down the whisper-quiet halls. We passed two empty viewing rooms, then a set of closed doors. Behind them, I could hear a man speaking.

Our journey continued beyond the offices and to an elevator.

"It will take two trips, or some of you can take the stairs," the director said.

"I'll go down the stairs," Corabelle said.

"You stay with the baby," Stella said to me. "I'll go down with Corabelle."

"You will be well taken care of," the director said, and shook my hand before heading back down the hall.

Mom and I filed into the elevator next to the trolley, the two men, and the woman from the other cemetery. The doors closed behind us.

We went down a floor. When the elevator opened, we were in another wide hall. A few chairs lined one side. At the end was another outside entrance, nothing fancy, just double doors that could open wide, and two metal doors to a room. Otherwise, it was one unbroken wall. The door to the stairs opened behind us and Stella and Corabelle rejoined us.

The woman's face remained placid and calm as she turned to us. "We're going into the crematorium now, where the casket will be opened and the baby prepared for cremation. You may go in, or you may wait out here." She gestured to the chairs.

Corabelle's face grew pale, but I could tell she would go in if she was asked.

"You all can just wait here," I said. "This might be hard."

Stella dropped into a chair and folded her hands in her lap. "We'll be right here," she said.

Corabelle sat beside her.

The men rolled the trolley forward to the metal doors. I followed behind them.

"Tina?" my mother asked.

I turned to her.

"I would like to come."

I hesitated. I wasn't sure I could manage if she got hysterical.

She came up beside me. "I'll be fine," she said.

I nodded. She linked her arm through mine. The men opened the metal doors and wheeled the casket through.

I braced myself. I could do this.

These rooms were clearly not intended for guests. Several workers in navy coveralls and black gloves manned large metal tables. A storeroom stood open, holding various styles of urns and a stack of plain boxes.

When they saw us, they nodded and moved aside.

The men rolled the trolley to the far side, where a table had been cleared. They lifted the casket onto it. One of them said, "We are very sorry for your loss," then rolled the trolley out again.

The woman stayed with us. "They will break the seal now," she told us. "Once they have done their work, they will let us know how to proceed."

Right. They had to approve our seeing Peanut. I wondered at the things they had seen. If they had managed, over time, to become numb to it.

The woman led us a little way away from the table as two of the workers approached the casket.

My mother gripped my arm like a vise. One of the men unlatched the side locks.

"They will break the seal now," the woman said.

The other man took a metal tool and slid it along the edges of the casket. The two of them struggled for a moment with the lid, then it came free.

But then they closed it again. Fear gripped me. Was it too much even for them?

The woman said, "They'll remove the hinges so the lid can come all the way off. It's easier to take him out that way."

I let out a long gust of air. I couldn't even cry now, I was so anxious.

One of the men walked to the other side of the casket to remove the hinges. The minutes were agonizing as he worked. I glanced over at Mother. Like me, she was rapt, probably both impatient and afraid of what they would find inside.

After what felt like an eternity, they lifted the lid completely away and set it aside. They looked down, then over at the woman, and nodded.

She stepped forward. "You can come over now," she said.

My feet had never felt heavier. I hadn't seen Peanut's face for seven years. Until a few weeks ago, I couldn't have imagined that I ever would again. I mentally flashed through all the grave-exhuming videos I had watched so I could prepare myself.

But when I peered inside, I could see only what I remembered. The small nubby nose. The tiny chin. Only his face showed above the blanket wrapped tightly around him. His skin was tight and mottled, but intact. I moved as if to reach in, but the man said, "Let's slide something beneath him first."

I pulled back. One of them held a flexible piece of clear plastic. He placed it inside the casket and shifted it beneath Peanut. I held my breath, knowing that they worried he would come apart. My mother stepped back, unable to watch. But when they lifted it, the blanket wrapped around him held.

They moved him to the table, carefully, with more tenderness than I would have expected from two gruff workers in coveralls. One of them tested the blanket and slid their hand beneath his body. He frowned.

But I didn't care. I opened the handkerchief my mother had given me and moved forward. The caretaker woman acted as if she might stop me, but I didn't give her that chance. I slid the handkerchief beneath him and folded it back over. He was so small. It was just the right size.

I wrapped the cloth tight so it would hold, and picked him up. He didn't feel much different from all those years ago. Light as air, but substantial and real. He still existed.

My mother walked up then and touched his forehead. "Sweet little bub," she said, tears flowing freely down her face. "He's still perfect."

I held him against me, wishing I could freeze this moment. I was such a different person now. I had to be. I couldn't fall apart at every setback life brought me. I had to be strong. I had so much to face. Surely, *surely*, this was the hardest thing I would ever do.

I pulled him close, my lips close to his ear. "You're going to be a big brother," I whispered. "Watch over us."

The caretaker approached. "You can walk him down," she said.

I followed her and one of the men to another area of the room. An enormous wall faced us with three steel doors. Leading up to each of them was a mechanized ramp.

A simple brown box sat on one ramp, about two feet long. I knew that was where Peanut would go.

I turned and let Mom see him one more time. She touched his forehead and stepped back again. I laid him in the box. I thought I would let the handkerchief go with him, but then changed my mind and unwrapped it from his body. I held it against my chest as I moved away.

The coveralls man fitted a lid onto the box and walked over to the metal door.

"Step back here," the caretaker woman said. She led Mom and me several feet from the ramp.

The man pressed a button and the metal door slid open. Inside I could see the orange light of the fire. Then he turned a switch and the ramp moved, taking the box inside.

I watched it go in and saw the flames alight on the box. Just as the fire began to burn brightly, the man closed the door.

Peanut was free.

22

JENNY

I was going to pace a hole in the floor. Phoenix was up on my shoulder, sleeping at last. I was afraid to put her down or she might wake up. She'd been fussing for hours. Growth spurt, maybe. Or a tooth coming in? She'd been drooling a lot.

My phone sat silent on the side table. I passed it, stopped, picked it up, saw nothing, and set it down again.

Corabelle was in Houston with Tina. Earlier today, they had taken her baby from his grave. I had no idea how that had gone, what state Tina was in, or when they were coming back. Or if Tina would.

I knew I was the wrong person to be out there. It wasn't right to have a baby in her face when she was going through all that.

But I felt so helpless.

The door opened and Chance strode in. I held my finger to my lips, and he turned to close it carefully.

I tried not to feel frumpy compared to him, me in my chenille robe and messy bun with hair flopping out. He looked every bit the rock star in faded jeans and a tight black T-shirt. His leather boots were tricked out with silver chains. It was just right. The stylist had changed his hair when they shot his album cover a week ago. Now the dark locks were cut short and spiked up in front.

He was seriously hot.

I tucked a piece of hair behind my ear and patted Phoenix's back. "Have fun at the Fire and Smash release party?"

"I'm not sure I'm sold on their sound, but there were good people there to chat up," Chance said. He came over and took Phoenix from me, transferring her to his shoulder. She stirred a little, but he resumed the patting and she settled down again.

I arched my back, relieved to have my arms free. "I've been watching the Tweets and shares from the party. Some killer shots of you with that Grammy-nominated singer — what was her name?"

His lips twisted. "That Cheri girl. Yeah, I had a hard time losing her tonight."

I laughed. "I saw. Every image had her fawning on your shoulder and you trying to look away."

He seemed relieved I was taking that well. And I would. Women were going to be throwing themselves at him constantly. I had to get used to that. I couldn't let it get to me. The moment I started to doubt him would be the day my fairy tale would end.

"So, you think she's down for a bit?" Chance asked. The rumble in his voice went straight to my belly.

"Go for the swing. Improves our odds."

He walked over to it and slowly, carefully, lowered Phoenix from his shoulder to the seat. I picked up a blanket thrown over the arm of the sofa and tucked it around her. Fate was on our side. She didn't wake.

Chance didn't wait for me to turn around, but put his hands on my hips and pulled me back against him.

"Somebody's fired up and ready," I said.

His fingers found the belt of my robe and untied it. "It's so much easier to get you naked these days," he said. "If I'm lucky, you'll never get fully dressed again."

"You'll keep me barefoot and pregnant?" I asked.

"I'm going to do my part." Her turned me around and tugged on the elastic band holding my hair, releasing it down my back. His fingers tangled into it as he drew me up to him.

I sighed into his lips as they lowered to mine. He smelled like wood smoke and aftershave. There must have been fire pits outside at the party.

"You taste so good," he said against my mouth. "Drinking coffee at midnight again."

"I wanted to stay up for you," I said. I hadn't been up for going. Prepping myself had seemed exhausting, and asking my mom to watch the baby until all hours wasn't fair on a weeknight.

"So glad you did." His hands slid inside the open robe. I had on simple cotton pajamas. Thankfully my boobs were cooperating these days and I wasn't milky all the time.

His fingers flirted with the bottom of my shirt, then slid upward. My lack of bra meant he found what he was looking for right off. I relaxed against him, reveling in the feel of his strong hands on me. There was nothing like him.

He broke the kiss and moved down, lifting my shirt higher so his mouth could find a nipple. I clutched at his head, savoring each sensation. He knew not to get too crazy and let my milk down. He got it just right.

His fingers grasped the elastic waistband of my pajama bottoms and let them fall. I shivered a little at the chill and he pulled me tighter against him.

Now his hands were everywhere, my hips, my back, clasping my behind. His breath was hot on my skin.

I was dying. I pulled his head away. "Let's go where I won't wake the baby," I said.

He gave me a wicked grin and stood, sweeping me up with him. The belt of my robe trailed along the floor as he carried me down the hall to the bedroom and closed the door.

I grabbed his neck and twisted in his arms until I was straddling him. I could feel him hard against me as we took the last few steps to the bed.

He bent forward to lay me down, dragging the robe away.

"Quickly, before she wakes up," I said, but he shushed me with a kiss. He wasn't going to be in a hurry.

He pulled my shirt over my head, breaking our connection to let the fabric pass between us. Then he made his way down, slowly, making me crazy with how he took his time.

He kissed a path down my collarbone, up the crest of one breast, then down to my belly button. He slid my panties down with a simple tug, then followed the newly exposed place until I arched up against his mouth.

His tongue teased me, circling the nub, until his fingers joined in. I quit thinking about the baby, or time, or the risk of her waking, and got lost in his work. Everything disappeared other than that pulsing need that was spiraling up and taking me over.

Chance knew me so well, reaching up to lightly tease a nipple, and I burst right over the edge, thrusting against him as I peaked, trying to contain my voice, hanging on to his shoulders for dear life.

I had barely caught my breath, still seeing lightning shards in my vision, when he grasped my hips and turned me over. I could hear his buckle jingle, and clothes hit the floor behind me.

Then his skin connected with mine, hot and rough. He slid inside me without any resistance. I dropped my head to the mattress, braced on my elbows, waiting for his first stroke.

When it came, I crashed back into him, taking him in hard. Chance groaned and sped up, holding tight to my hips.

For long moments he worked me, keeping a strong rhythm, then reached around for me again.

My hair was everywhere, flowing across the bed. When he touched me, I lurched back again. I was so hot, so full of need.

His fingers worked me, and I tightened around him. He felt me go and unleashed inside me, pulsing as I muffled this second round of cries in the blankets.

When he was spent, we stayed there a moment, breathing hard, trying to find our bearings. Chance's arms came around me, lifting me against him, my back to his chest. I stayed there, loving the strong arms around me, until my thighs quaked, and he lay both of us down across the bed.

We stayed there a while in the quiet when I heard, in the distance, my phone chime with Corabelle's ringtone. It was late to be hearing from her.

"I don't think I can get that," I told Chance.

He chuckled. "That's one of your girlfriends, right?"

"Corabelle. She's in Houston with Tina."

"Seems like you'd want that call." He shifted away from me

and headed toward the living room.

He came back, my phone pressed to his ear. "She's right here," he said, passing the phone to me.

"Is everything okay?" I asked. The cold hit right about then, and I shivered. Chance covered me with my robe and kissed the back of my head. I mouthed a silent "Thank you."

"Today was tough," she said. "We moved the baby from the grave to the crematorium. I didn't go back when they opened the casket, but Tina said he was fine. She held him."

"Whoa." I tried to picture this, but couldn't do it. "Is she all right?"

"Yeah. The ashes will be ready tomorrow to pick up."

"Is she coming back?"

Corabelle sighed. "I don't think so. She's got an artist studio she's renting and seems pretty set on staying a while."

"What about Darion?"

"She won't talk about him. Or Albert. She just diverts the conversation to other things."

I tugged the robe around me. Chance headed to the bathroom. "Can't you do anything?"

"I think I've done all I can. It's not up to us. But she is okay. She's got a friend or two here."

"So, we've lost her?"

The phone was silent for a moment.

Then finally Corabelle said, "I think we have."

23

TINA

I had forgotten how Houston exploded with azaleas in the spring.

The dead-looking bushes surrounding the greenhouses at the artist studio had burst with color practically overnight. There must be some weather condition, or timing of the sun, that made them all know when to show up at once.

That morning when I saw them, I stopped futzing around with the cemetery image and started painting flowers. I hadn't been able to do solid work for a week, and the blooms were like a fresh start.

Sarah, the woman who owned the studio, popped into the greenhouse to check on a section of glass that had been replaced the day before. The artist who had been sharing the space with me had gone on a rampage after a bad review of his gallery opening and thrown his metal stool right through one of the panes.

He'd been kicked out.

"Good as new," she said, patting the glass. "And good riddance." She stood and straightened her straw hat. She looked like a strawberry, in pink cropped pants and a patterned shirt. Well, a skinny strawberry. Her veined ankles stood out above her black Crocs. She had to be seventy.

I laughed. "He was a cliché, wasn't he? The brooding, unpredictable *artiste*."

"A menace, that's what he was. And a mess." She rubbed her foot on an oil-paint stain that hadn't come off the concrete floor when she cleared out his stuff.

"But now you're out the rent." I stuck my watercolor brush in a glass of water.

"I'll get by," she said. "How's the work coming?"

"Been inspired by the flowers," I said. "I've never really done landscapes."

She peered over my shoulder and nodded. "Awful cheerful for you. Must be the baby."

My hand flew to my belly. I wasn't even close to showing. It had only been three weeks since Stella figured it out. "How?"

"We old women know a thing or two," she said. "Besides, you threw up in the sunflower bed two days ago."

I had. Stella and I had gone for pasta, which had seemed safe enough until I got out of her car.

"I thought it was just a patch of weeds," I said ruefully.

"A common mistake," Sarah said. "The stalks and leaves aren't much without the blooms. Sort of like the azaleas." She walked over to the glass wall and looked out on the riot of color outside. "So dead looking other than these few glorious weeks. But worth it." She turned back to my easel. "Especially when someone with talent makes them immortal."

I fiddled with the brushes, hoping she wouldn't go back to the topic of the baby. Other than picking up a bottle of prenatal vitamins, I hadn't thought much about the pregnancy. I had no doubt the condition was temporary. Twenty weeks, early labor, and another set of ashes.

Pessimism was my muse.

Except maybe today. The pinks and purples called to me. Colorful. Happy. Something lovely blossoming from nothing but sticks.

Sarah perched on the other stool. "I couldn't help but notice that the checks you write have a California address. Is that home?"

My cheeks burned. "I'm living with my parents right now here in Houston." I didn't care what she thought of that, if I was unable to make it on my own.

I guessed my tone told her I didn't want to discuss it, because she stood up and straightened her hat. "I'm sure they are happy to have you around again. I haven't seen my daughter in three years. Busy life she has."

My heart squeezed. Sarah was just lonely. "You should call her. Don't wait for her to call you. She probably remembers, but never at a time when she can do it."

"Wise words," Sarah said. "You keep on with those azaleas. That will be a lovely painting to hang somewhere that needs a bit of cheer." She hesitated. "And about the baby — bearing a child is the ultimate expression of hope. You may think you are filled with despair, but your flowers give you away."

She headed out of the greenhouse. I stared at the canvas. It was so unlike anything I'd ever done, even when doing paintings in college. I had always managed to twist the assignment into something dark. Floral arrangement? Black roses. Portrayal of the divinity? Crucifixion. Still life of food? Rotten fish.

But not today.

I picked up the brush. Sarah had forced me to think about the baby. Stella had kept her word and told no one. Corabelle hadn't guessed. But if two women had figured it out, no doubt my mother would soon.

Damn.

I mingled more magenta into the shadow side of the flowers, but my head was elsewhere. I stuck the brush back in the water. On an impulse, I picked up my phone. I sent Darion one text message a day, something easy, about the paintings or my mother or a complaint about traffic or weather.

But today, I said, "Might be time for us to talk."

I waited a minute or two, worried that he might have given up on me. I was difficult and moody and sad. I'd left him.

As the minutes stretched on, I tried to reassure myself. He was on rounds. He couldn't check his phone. He'd text me back.

But anxiety prickled. I'd blown it. He was done. I'd gone too far, leaving like this and not wanting to talk to him.

Then a message beeped. I scrambled to pull it up, my heart in my throat.

Just bought a plane ticket. Arrive in four hours.

I almost dropped the phone. So, he wanted to talk in person. For the first time in the six weeks I had been gone, I felt a soaring sensation inside. Darion was coming.

24

CORABELLE

Tina's text was simple.

Thanks for coming to Houston. Darion headed here. Be home soon.

I stood in the middle of the pharmacy near my apartment, my shoulders shaking from holding in my tears. She would return. She was better.

One of my biggest fears was that she and I would never recover from our losses. That the hole would be too big to ever fill. We'd never move on.

But Tina was doing it.

I could do it.

I plucked a bottle of shampoo off the shelf and dropped it into my basket. Gavin was already much better from his vasectomy reversal, and our follow-up appointment was in three weeks. Then we'd know where we stood.

I wouldn't be afraid.

Two girls passed, giggling, with a box of condoms. Good for them, I thought, then paused by the sign that said "Family Planning."

I took a few steps closer to the pregnancy tests. I didn't see the one I had taken all those years ago, when I found out I was having Finn. They must have changed the design. I couldn't remember the brand.

Below them were ovulation predictors. You could buy individual sticks, or splurge and pick up a little computer that told you the best time to try to get pregnant.

It was a crazy price, really, plus you had to buy little test strips to put in it.

But I put it in my basket.

And in a few weeks, I might get to try this gadget out.

I refused to feel any guilt about the money as I checked out and drove home. You couldn't put a dollar figure on hope.

When I pulled into the parking lot of the complex, Gavin was just getting off his motorcycle.

He seemed extra animated as he removed his helmet and came over to take the bag from me.

"What's going on?" I said, already smiling from the extra energy coming off him.

"I'll have to show you," he said. "You got your laptop?"

"It's in my backpack," I said. "You have a paper due?" Gavin was still in one night class.

"No. It's something amazing," he said.

I followed him up to the door, wondering what was going on.

He set the bag on the coffee table and lifted the backpack

from my shoulders. "Come here," he said, sitting on the sofa. He pulled the laptop out.

"You going to tell me?" I asked.

"Only if I need tech help." His grin was huge, like he couldn't contain his excitement.

He pulled out his phone to consult something, then opened a video chat window on the laptop.

"You going to Skype?" I asked.

"Yup," he said.

"Who with?" I couldn't imagine he would be this excited about anybody, certainly not his parents.

But when I saw the number he was putting in, I knew. International call.

"Manuelito," I said.

He waited a second, hands clasped, impatient, and then the call went through. Rosa came on the screen.

"Hello again," she said. "Hello, Corabelle."

I looked over at Gavin. "You found her?"

"The investigator got something into the compound. She called at the garage. I couldn't talk then."

Rosa moved aside, and Manuelito filled the screen, so close we could see only his eyes and nose.

"Papa Gavin!" he said. "Corbell!"

Tears sprang for the second time that day. "Hey, baby," I said.

"We got your number again!" Manuelito said. "Finally!"

Gavin said, "They took Rosa's phone with all her contact numbers when she arrived. Really tight security there."

I wanted to ask him what it was all about, but Manuelito backed up and we could see more of him.

"You cut your hair," Gavin said. The boy's thick black mop was burred close to his head.

Manuelito ran his hand over it. "It's fuzzy!" he said. "And look!" He turned and pointed to a lightning bolt shaved on the side.

"Wow!" Gavin said.

"Mama Rosa let me do it. Now I'm like Bolt!"

"Just like in the movie," I said.

"I've missed you," Gavin said.

"Me too!" Manuelito said. "It's been forever!"

I clasped Gavin's hand. "Papa Gavin went to Mexico looking for you."

Rosa's face entered the frame. "I know, Gavinito," she said. "I am sorry. I did not know where we were going until we got here, and then they took everything. I should have memorized your numbers."

"When can I see him?" Gavin asked.

She pulled Manuelito onto her lap. "I will try, Gavin. We are safe here. That is all I can say."

"What is going on?" he asked.

She shook her head. "Family trouble. I can say no more. But if I can come, I will come. You can call us whenever you like now. We are not prisoners. Just safe."

I squeezed Gavin's hand.

"Can I come there?" he asked.

"No, please, no," she said. "It will not always be like this. But for now, it must be. I will try to come to you by summer. Please understand, Gavin."

"I don't understand," he said.

"I am so sorry," she said. "We have to go now. We will talk

again, anytime you like, okay?"

Gavin nodded. There was nothing else he could do. "Bye, buddy," he said to Manuelito. "You be good for Mama Rosa, okay?"

Manuelito waved. "Bye-bye! Love you!" His little-boy enthusiasm was not dampened by the tension between the adults.

"Love you too, Little Bud," Gavin said.

Rosa reached forward and ended the call.

I leaned against Gavin. We both stared at the empty video box. "What do you think is going on?" I asked.

"Probably that cousin," he said. "You know he disappeared last year. That's why Rosa contacted me in the first place. No telling what he's into."

"You think they are safe?" I asked. "She said they were, but who knows?"

He rocked his head back on the cushions to stare at the ceiling. "They seem happy enough."

"Summer isn't far. Just a couple months."

"If she really comes."

We were so helpless. But at least he knew where Manuelito was. He was back in our lives. That was a start.

25

TINA

Waking up next to Darion again was like a small miracle. I had told myself I had not missed him, that the pressure of a relationship was too much. But now I knew. I belonged here.

We had gone to a hotel. I couldn't handle taking him to the little garage apartment behind my parents' house. My life had fallen apart there too many times.

I thought he was still asleep as I turned to him, a strip of sunlight coming through a gap in the blackout curtains crossing his cheek. But then I saw him move and realized his eyes were open.

"Hello, sunshine," he said.

"You talking to the window or to me?" I asked.

He laughed and drew me tight against him. His arms were strong and his chest smooth. I had forgotten how it felt to be surrounded by him, protected.

Sheltered.

We hadn't talked about anything important yet. He'd gotten in much later than planned, due to plane delays. We'd had a quiet dinner and come to the hotel. He hadn't assumed anything, but of course, being us, things got physical fast.

I hadn't told him about the baby.

Luckily, I didn't feel too nauseated, so there was no telltale puking to clue him in. Although, when I turned down a glass of wine last night, Darion had tilted his head, a question in his eyes. I had only shrugged. So he might have figured it out.

We both knew my shot was way overdue. We'd agreed back before Albert died that I didn't have to go back on it. We had every intention of having a tiny wedding at the JP's office, and it could happen anytime.

I'd been coasting for a whole year, letting things happen rather than *making* them happen.

"Did you get Peanut's ashes?" he asked. His fingers slid through the tangles in my hair.

"I did. They're at my mother's house. I put some in my necklace, though, with Albert's."

"Do I get to meet her?" he asked.

"Sure," I said.

Definitely time for that. Time for a lot of things. A doctor visit, for one. Make sure the baby was okay. Confessing. Maybe I should do that one now.

"So, Darion…" I faltered. I felt crushed by my deceit. I had known I was pregnant for weeks, since Stella said it and I confirmed it with a test. But I'd kept the knowledge of his own child from him.

My stomach flipped and the nausea came on full force. I didn't throw up often, which is why I'd ended up in Sarah's sunflowers the other day, but I might right now.

I took a deep breath in, trying to calm myself. My nerves were probably making it worse.

"Tina?" Darion's voice was edged with concern.

I sat up, holding the sheet to my chest. Leaving the warmth of him made me feel even sicker, and I shuddered. He sat up and drew me back against him. I relaxed as our skin connected once more.

"I haven't told you something important," I said. "And it was awful of me…" I stopped again. I'd screwed up big-time. Darion wasn't the type to get angry, but he'd be so disappointed that I didn't tell him. That I couldn't pull myself out of my own self-centered mire of misery to think about how he might feel.

His hand slid along my ribs and down to my belly. "I'm a doctor, remember? I know a pregnant uterus when I feel it. I'm glad you got some time to yourself with this little one. You weren't alone."

I lost it then, hot tears falling on his shoulder. I felt everything at once. Relief. Intense admiration. Love. This man was willing to sacrifice anything to let me do what I needed to. I'd put off our wedding. Deserted my job. Obsessed over an artist friend. And then left him without a word.

Yet, he was here, explaining to me how it had been exactly the right thing to do.

"I think I might love you, Dr. Marks," I said. My face was crushed against his chest.

"That's a good thing, then," he said. "Because I don't think I could have stayed away much longer."

"I won't go away again," I said.

"Sure you will," he teased, his fingers stroking my neck.

"You'll take off to paint Niagara Falls or an African jungle and leave me with an infant in a baby sling and a freezer full of breast milk."

I choked out a laugh. "I might, actually. You sure you're up for this?"

Darion kissed the top of my head. "I have been since the day we met."

~*'`*~

Darion pulled up to my parents' house that afternoon, and I steeled myself. I'd given up on finding something in common with my mother. But we were talking again. I didn't know what I'd expected coming here. Certainly not that we'd be chummy friends, shopping for jeans that didn't make our butts look big. But something.

I didn't really know how to do this daughter thing.

Mom opened the door before we even got out of the car. She stepped onto the porch, my father behind her. He must have come back sometime this week. I hadn't been in the main house in a few days, sneaking off early in the morning and returning late.

Like a teenager, I realized. Maybe I hadn't grown up at all.

Mom enveloped me in a huge hug when we got to them. Dad shook Darion's hand.

"You must be the doctor we've heard so much about," Dad said.

I raised an eyebrow at him over Mom's shoulder. I hadn't said much at all to them about Darion.

"Nice to meet you, sir," Darion said.

Now the teenager in me was really coming out, because I

snorted. Sir? Darion was in his thirties! He didn't have to call anyone sir.

Mom let go of me and turned to Darion. "I'm so happy you're here."

We went inside. When we had settled on Mom's hideous floral sofas, she asked, "Are you going to stay a while?"

Darion answered without hesitation. "I have my rounds covered for a couple days. Then I do have to get back." He took my hand. "You've been such a comfort for Tina that she'll have to decide for herself whether she's ready to leave or not."

He was good. Mom beamed at him.

"A little early for a cocktail," Dad said, "but we do have some beer."

"I'm fine, thank you," Darion said.

Dad sat down, and I figured that was it. End of any conversation or common ground. We could not be more different from the two people who had raised me, Mom in her cotton dress, and Dad in his business casual even at home.

But Darion was on it. "So, when did Tina start painting? She's quite good."

Mom was perfectly happy to prattle on about my whole history of art. I started feeling sleepy partway through her spiel, but Darion was attentive and alert.

"Let me go find some of her finger paintings," my mom said, standing up.

I held out my hand. "That isn't necessary," I said. "We've probably got more pressing issues."

She sat back down, sending a concerned look at my father.

Darion took my hand. When I didn't speak up, he did. "We're

still in the planning stages of the wedding. I'm sure you'll want to come out for that."

"Just a JP thing," I said quickly.

Darion nodded. "But I'm sure they'll want to be there. Along with my father and sister, and I believe you met Corabelle."

"She was a delightful girl," Mom said. "Went to so much trouble to come down."

"She is," Darion said. His eyes met mine, as if to ask, *anything else?*

"And I'm pregnant," I blurted out. "So, we'll probably do the wedding sooner rather than later."

Mom sucked in a sharp breath.

"Well, then," Dad said. "Maybe we should have that cocktail after all." He got up and headed to the liquor cabinet.

This made me laugh out loud. "Really, Dad?"

Darion pulled me close to his side. "We're not very far along. And we'll make sure we have the best specialists watching for another cervical issue or premature labor."

Mom was pale. "Do you think it could happen again?"

"I've looked into the issue pretty thoroughly since Tina told me about Peanut," Darion said.

This was news to me. He had on his doctor face, the one that assures parents of kids with cancer that they are doing everything possible.

It was a good face.

"It's a pretty simple stitch that they place around her cervix," Darion said. "It's very effective in keeping everything closed during the high-growth period of the baby's gestation." He looked at me warmly. "I'll personally oversee everything that is done."

"Oh, Tina, how lucky you are to have a doctor watching you now." My mom rushed over to me and pulled me to her in an awkward hug. "It's going to be just fine. I know it." She released me to turn to my dad. "We're going to have to fly out for the wedding, and then again when the baby is due. We can find a place to rent for a few weeks. If we skip our vacation this year, we'll be able to swing that."

They talked excitedly about their plans. For a moment, I felt regret that I'd come here and involved them. They'd be all up in my life again, just like when I lived here.

Darion accepted a drink from Dad and they shook hands. Mom embraced him. I watched all this, feeling awkward and weird. They liked him. They liked my life.

And that's when I realized, this is what family does. It's not about being chums or having long talks or common interests or even understanding each other.

Being part of a family is about showing up, no matter how hard it gets. It's about knowing that somebody will always just plain *be there*.

26

CORABELLE

Jenny shook the spray can of colored glitter and aimed it at the table. "You know, Corabelle, we've all got a habit of getting knocked up before we're married."

I took the can from her before she got it everywhere and spread newspapers down. My best friend had the common sense of a grasshopper, but I loved her.

"Well, it seems to work out in the end," I said. "Sometimes it takes some effort, but it works out."

"You had it the worst," she said. "I just had to search all over Tennessee. You had to wait four years. Imagine if Gavin hadn't taken that astronomy class."

"I think about it every day," I said.

Phoenix babbled from her swing. I had come over to Jenny's to finish the decorations for Tina's wedding. We'd talked her out of going to the courthouse and were setting up an arch and some chairs on a cliff she said was important to her. Apparently some things between her and Darion went down at that spot. Duct tape was involved.

I hadn't asked questions.

"I'm glad we're getting more use out of these stars you made," Jenny said. "Although I don't see why they couldn't have stayed pink."

"Tina's not big on pink."

Jenny set one of the cardboard stars on the newspaper and aimed her spray glitter again. "Well, the rainbow has pink in it."

I shook my head. Jenny was funny. We were doing our best to make the stars multicolored. Stella had said babies born after a loss were called rainbow babies, the beauty after the rain. And Tina had always worn rainbow-striped stockings when she was pregnant before, so it all fit.

The spray made a loud hissing sound, startling the baby, who began to cry. Jenny put down the can and headed over to her.

I guessed the stars were my job again.

I quickly added a section of green to each of the five stars, one large, two medium, and two small. They would hang from the arch over Tina and Darion. I was hoping to keep them from looking tacky or amateur. Darion could do any sort of wedding he wanted, but I guessed the personal homespun version appealed to them. Maybe it reminded him of his own mother. I was sad for both of them that she was no longer with them to see this day.

Gavin had not invited his parents to ours. One day we'd mend that breach. But if his father hadn't changed, if he was still the angry, abusive person we'd known growing up, I could see why Gavin would keep him away. His sister would grow up eventually, and I'd make sure we had a relationship with her. Family was important.

I switched to blue and added another stripe to each star. They were turning out pretty nice, I thought, blending together in a smooth band of color.

Jenny approached, Phoenix on her shoulder. The baby was six months old now and almost sitting up. She beamed at me in that happy smile only older babies could do. The tiny bit of tooth gleamed from her gum. They grew so fast.

I pressed my hand against my belly self-consciously, and Jenny noticed.

"Taken a test yet?" she asked.

"Too soon," I said.

"For you or for testing?"

I shrugged. "I'll do it when I can handle it."

"Worried there weren't enough swimmers?"

I picked up the can of orange glitter paint. "His count was low, for sure," I said. "We might not be able to conceive naturally. But we'll just let what happens, happens. That's why we're not preventing, even though I'm still in school. Later on we will be able to afford in vitro or whatever we need to do."

Jenny set Phoenix on a blanket on the floor, arranging her in the tripod position with her legs out and arms in the middle. The baby managed to sit for a few seconds before toppling over.

"You'll get it, baby boo," Jenny said. She put her on her tummy with a toy and surveyed my work. "You're doing better than I would."

I was on the last color. "I like it." I shook the can and sprayed some purple on. "Might need a little more green."

Jenny pointed to the largest star. "Yeah, on that one

especially."

I focused on the stars. Jenny moved away. I finished the purple and added a bit more green. That was it.

Jenny came back and stuck something close to my face. I moved back a step. "What is that?"

When I focused in, I saw it was a pregnancy test.

"Are you knocked up again already?" I asked.

"No, silly! It's unused. One of my leftovers from Phoenix." She waved it at me. "Come on. Let's do it."

"I couldn't. Not without Gavin."

She leaned against the table. "Now, think about it. I told you before I told Chance."

"Because you didn't know his last name!"

She held up her palm. "Details. And Tina's friends in Houston knew before Darion."

"What's your point, Jenny?"

"I'm just saying that our girl circle clues in our dudes after the fact. Besties before testes."

I snorted a laugh. "Did you really just say that?"

"I did!" she said. "Come on!" She waved it in front of me again. "I gotta know. I just gotta know."

I looked at the test. I wasn't even late yet, although I knew those tests could tell you a couple days before.

Was I ready to find out? This was the first month we'd tried. We knew the odds were against us.

I should wait for Gavin.

I should just wait.

But I took the stick.

"Yes!" Jenny cried. Phoenix looked up from her blanket, her

face perplexed at her mother's exuberance. Jenny scooped her up. "You're going to have a playmate!"

"Maybe," I said. Now that I held the test in my hand, my belly was tightening with fear.

"I'll hold your hand," Jenny said. "Let's go make some pee."

"It's not first-morning urine," I said. "It might not be valid."

"Not listening!" Jenny said. "Less talking, more peeing!"

"You going to come into the bathroom with me?" I asked.

"Damn straight," she said. "I'm not letting you chicken out."

What had I gotten myself into?

Still, Jenny's excitement was pretty catching. As she walked, she bounced the baby, who giggled infectiously.

I decided to just get it over with. A negative wouldn't really mean anything, between being a day or two early and not using the best urine. I could handle it.

Jenny hopped up on the cabinet next to the sink and held Phoenix in her lap. "This is how you know you are real besties," she told the baby. "If you pee on pregnancy sticks together."

She went on to tell the baby about how she called me when she got scared, and I tuned her out as I focused on the stick. I hadn't done this in a long time.

At first, I couldn't make anything come out with Jenny watching, but she noticed and turned away. Then she turned on the water faucet.

When the stream hit the stick, panic coursed through me again. Why was I doing this now? I needed Gavin. I needed to think.

I wouldn't look.

I capped the end and set it aside. By the time I had washed my hands, I was positive I'd done the wrong thing. "I'm going to head home," I told Jenny. "I don't want to know anything right now."

Jenny frowned and hopped off the cabinet. "Okay, Corabelle. I'm sorry. I thought it would be fun."

I headed to the living room and picked up my bag. "Those stars should be dry tonight. It doesn't take long, but watch for any wet spots."

Jenny's face contorted like she was going to make a remark about wet spots, but I shot her a glare. She sobered up and shifted Phoenix on her hip. "I won't look, Corabelle. I'll just toss it."

I shrugged and headed for the front door. "I can pick the stars up tomorrow. Gavin and I will be the ones setting up the arch and chairs."

"Okay. Thanks for coming over to help," she said.

I waved good-bye and walked to the car. I would put the pregnancy test from my mind. In a few days, if I didn't get my period, Gavin and I would test together.

The day was warm and breezy. Spring was well underway and school would be out in a few weeks, although I was staying on through the summer. I had been doubling up and would finish my master's degree in record time. I had only a few classes to go and then my thesis. Hopefully my professors would recommend me, and I could start teaching as an adjunct next year. I had the experience as a TA already.

My future was coming.

I pulled out my phone and called Gavin. Rosa was supposed to let him know today if she could make it to the States. We had lots of plans for things to do with Manuelito, and focusing on that would help take my mind off pregnancy tests and trying-not-trying.

He picked up on the second ring. "Did you hear from Rosa?" I asked.

"Yes," he said. "Looks like we're on for mid-June."

"I'm so glad, Gavin. It will be good to see him."

I heard footsteps behind me. I turned. Jenny was coming at me in a full sprint, Phoenix bobbing on her hip.

"Corabelle! Corabelle!" she shouted.

"Hold on, Gavin, Jenny's running at me. We've been making Tina's wedding stars." I turned to her. She'd arrived, breathing hard.

"What is it?" I asked.

She held out the stick. "I lied. I looked."

I took it from her.

Faint, just barely there, was a thin red line next to the control line.

"Two lines," she said. "It's there."

My knees gave out and I sat on the grass by the curb.

"Corabelle," Gavin said through the phone. "Everything okay?"

I couldn't find my voice just yet. I would in a minute. I stared at the stick. I could see everything in that pale, pale line. My future. My fear. My love.

But mainly, I saw hope.

27

TINA

I had definitely picked the perfect spot for the wedding.

The air was salty and a gentle breeze stirred the stars Corabelle had repainted from Jenny's shower. The arch was almost invisible, white against the white clouds. Beyond it, the sea stretched into the horizon, as if infinity itself was in attendance.

In the dozen or so chairs angled toward the cliff's edge were all the people who mattered. Corabelle and Gavin, Manuelito on his lap. Jenny and Chance, who was jiggling Phoenix to keep her quiet. Stella.

Layla sat in the back row with an empty seat we had reserved in memory of Albert. I bit my lip for a moment, trying to rein in my emotions. Jenny would kill me if I messed up her careful makeup job.

I took a few steps back so I was hidden behind a bush. My father and I waited at the top of the trail for Darion's little sister to arrive, signaling that Darion and his father were in place. The breeze stirred the gauzy skirt of my dress, lifting the lightweight fabric so that it brushed my knees.

I looked down at my stockings, the gold and silver stripes so subtle that it appeared my legs were simply white. I passed the bouquet of pastel roses to my father for a moment so I could straighten the crazy complicated bodice of the dress, a million seed pearls sewn onto a corset. It gave me the illusion of having boobs and made a nice straight line over my just-starting-to-pop belly. I assumed the boobs would come later or Junior was going to be seriously malnourished.

The pregnancy was going fine. Now that the second trimester had begun, I felt a lot less sick. The cervical stitch was in, a little wire loop that kept things shut tight until it was time to deliver. I was calm. Well, as calm as anyone could be on their wedding day.

"You look perfect," Dad said. "Never a bride any prettier than you."

I gave him a nervous smile and took the bouquet back. He tucked my hand inside the crook of his arm.

Darion's nine-year-old sister, Cynthia, popped out from behind a bush. "Time to go!" she said. She was adorable and pixie-like in her vivid blue dress.

I peered back down the trail. She was right. The JP was in place under the arch, and Darion and his dad were just walking up to stand beside him.

"Where's Mom?" I asked.

"Right here!" she said, picking her way down the trail. "Had to pin the boutonniere on your boy!"

My heart squeezed that she was standing in at least a little for

Darion's mom, who had died so many years ago. "Thank you."

"I'm so excited!" she said. "I never got to be a maid of honor before! And here I am, at my ripe old age."

"You're not old, Mom," I said. "And you look great."

"Thank you for not going with a pastel," she said. She swished the skirt of her sapphire dress. "I'm going to go out dancing in this number."

"You'll knock everybody's socks off," Dad said.

Mom blushed.

"The officiant is waving at us," Dad said. "I think it's time."

Cynthia jumped in the air with excitement. "I'm going!" She struck out down the trail, picking flower petals from her basket and dropping them in the dirt.

Mom waited a few moments, then followed her.

Dad squeezed my arm. "This is one of the happy days," he said. "Savor as much of it as you can."

"I will, Dad," I said.

As we headed up the trail, the solo violinist began to play, a lovely sweet song that Darion's mother had written when he was young. It had words, but we didn't ask anyone to sing. Cynthia had said she'd be too nervous.

But when we arrived at the chairs, I realized she had changed her mind, because she was standing by Darion, belting out the chorus.

Love is tender, love is tough
Don't ever think you've had enough

I bent to kiss the top of her elaborate hairdo and stood to one side of her as Dad left me to go sit in the chairs. When the song ended, Darion gave her a hug and whispered, "Thank you." She moved into her place between him and their father.

I passed my bouquet to my mom and turned to Darion. This was it.

He looked amazing in a traditional black tux with a tie that matched my mother's dress. The breeze ruffled his dark hair. My stomach fluttered. I was getting *married*. Me. This was crazy.

I must have looked uncertain, because Darion took my hands and lifted them both to his lips. "I love you," he said quietly. "Besides, you can probably have it annulled tomorrow."

The JP, who had taken in a deep breath to start the ceremony, let out a gush of air instead. "Really?" he asked.

I laughed. "I'm a little gun-shy," I said. "But I think this one is going to stick."

The JP looked back and forth between us for a moment, as if waiting to see if we were really going to do this. When neither of us made a run for it, he said, "We have gathered here today for the marriage of Tina Schwartz and Dr. Darion Marks."

I lifted an eyebrow at the "doctor." Darion tilted his head in his father's direction. I nodded in understanding and rolled my eyes. Titles. They were important to the senior Dr. Marks.

The JP cleared his throat. We both snapped to attention. We hadn't heard a word he had said.

"You are supposed to be repeating after me," he said.

"Sorry," Darion said. "I couldn't take my eyes off my wife."

The guests tittered.

The JP began again, "I, Darion, take Tina to be my lawfully wedded wife," he said.

Darion gripped my fingers. When he met my gaze this time, my breath caught with his intensity and emotion. "I, Darion, take Tina to be my lawfully wedded wife."

"To have and to hold," the JP said.

"You know," Darion said, and everyone laughed again. "I think I can handle this part on my own. Is that all right?"

The JP smiled and stepped back. "By all means."

My heart smashed against my chest. What was he doing?

Darion took a step closer.

"Tina Schwartz, I promise to pay attention to you and to recognize when you need space, or time, or a new canvas, or more Cerulean Blue Blick oil paint because you're stealing all of mine."

I had to smile. It was true. I always ran out of that color first.

"And I'll give you it," he said. "And if I can, I'll see it coming and give it to you before you even know you need it. Because you are something incredible, beyond anything or anyone I've ever known. And the work of your hands, because it comes from the understanding in your heart, is going to speak to people. And I want to be the person who helps you get there."

I felt dumbstruck. He had spoken to my hopes and my fears all in one. He knew what I wanted before I could even form the words myself.

"I will also change diapers," he said with a huge, beautiful grin.

"Get it in writing," Jenny said from her chair, elbowing Chance. Everyone burst into laughter.

I let go of him to wipe a tear from the corner of my eye and took his hand again. He looked down at me with earnestness and love.

"And I, Tina Schwartz, take you, Dr. Darion Marks, to be my

lawfully wedded husband, and not just because you knocked me up before we could tie the knot." I waited out the laughs.

"But because you know me better than I know myself. You see in me the things I have not dared to stare in the face. Because you are the best thing to ever happen to me. And because I've gone without you and I never want to have to do that again."

He lifted my knuckles to his lips.

The JP stepped back. "Do we have rings?"

Cynthia jumped forward. "I do!" She dug around in her basket and produced a small silk bag. "In here!"

Darion released me to take the sack from her. He opened it and let the wedding bands fall into his palm. He handed them to the officiant.

"This is the easy part," the man said. He gave the smaller ring to Darion. "Place this on her finger and say, 'With this ring, I thee wed.'" He hesitated. "Unless you have more to say."

Darion's strong hand lifted mine. He caressed my finger before sliding the band onto it. "With this ring, I thee wed."

I took the band from the officiant and reached for Darion. His hands were warm. I slid the ring onto his finger. "With this ring, I thee wed," I said.

"By the power vested in me by the State of California," the JP said, "I now pronounce you husband and wife. Tina, you may kiss your husband."

This got another laugh.

Darion held my hand against his heart for a moment, just watching me. I remembered that day we came here and I envisioned the painting of me and Peanut. I'd been obsessed with the need to capture that feeling, the emotion that surged inside me thinking about what it would be like if he were with me. The urge to paint my emotions was strong whenever I was moved to feel something bigger than myself.

Everything that had happened to me since he died, the anger at my parents, the escape from Houston to art school, the one-night stands, the urgency to always move on, had all come from that one day my life had fallen apart.

Albert knew this too. He'd gotten stuck, endlessly painting clowns that made him famous but never let him get past his one terrible heartbreak.

I wouldn't make the same mistake.

I knew now I would never finish that painting on the cliff. I had a new memory here. This day with Darion. I pressed my hand against my belly. I would not get stuck. I would move forward. I would never forget Peanut. That wasn't possible. But I wouldn't let that one tragedy, no matter how great, define me. I was more than that. I had so much more life to live, endless paths to explore.

I got it now. Happily ever after wasn't a destination at all.

It was a journey.

Darion had waited long enough for his kiss, and he leaned in to brush his lips against mine. I could hear the cheers from everybody I loved and who loved me, right there on this cliff.

The wind picked up, and Darion's finger touched my cheek. I pulled back from him, just an inch, and looked up into his eyes. My future was right in front of me.

I took his hand and led him to the edge of the cliff, a few feet beyond the arch. Like our wedding vows, this part wasn't scripted. There was no repeating other people's words, other weddings' sentiments. This moment was all our own.

I grasped the shell necklace and pulled hard, snapping the fragile chain. Darion frowned, lifting his hand to catch it. "You broke it," he said.

I nodded. I held the locket in my hands. Below, the ground fell away to the sea, waves crashing below. I felt I knew every boulder and tree after attempting to paint it so many times.

My fingernail slid into the locket's clasp and flipped it up.

Darion knew what I was doing and cupped his hands beneath mine. I flicked the locket open and the wind caught the ashes.

They spiraled up a moment, just a puff against the open sky. Albert and Peanut, airborne, a soft cloud against the Blick Cerulean Blue.

Then, just as quickly, they dissipated, disappearing into the light. Gone.

Darion's hands tightened on mine. Behind me, Corabelle came up and placed her arm around my shoulders. Then Jenny. Then my mom. Then Layla.

We looked out onto the sea from the cliff. The violin played again, a gentle tune, and I knew, without a doubt, that I was ready for whatever came next.

Epilogue

GAVIN

The three girls were all sitting at the water's edge. Jenny's daughter, Phoenix, was the big kid, toddling along, falling face-first in the sand, getting up, and doing it all over again.

I elbowed Chance. "I see where she gets her coordination."

He shook his head and stuck his hat back down over his eyes. He'd been up half the night at some rock-star party and was seriously not thrilled about being out before noon. Tough life. I didn't feel one bit sorry for him.

The doc was digging through the cooler, probably looking for something healthier than the pastrami on rye I was eating. He occasionally looked up to watch Tina with their baby, who was big enough to sit up, laughing her head off every time a wave came in and touched her feet.

"Give it up," I said. "Eat crap and drink beer."

He held up a bag of carrots like it was a gold nugget he'd

personally cut from a mine. "Never surrender," he said.

Corabelle tried sticking Ethan's feet in the water, but the minute the cold touched his toes, he seized up like a frog and screamed. He was two months old and had definitely discovered how to get people to act fast.

"Your kid has some lungs," Darion said, plunking back down in the sand. "I bet he keeps you up at night."

I could hear his wails over the waves. "I've got three words for you, Doc. Noise. Canceling. Headphones."

Darion laughed. "Smart man."

Corabelle lifted Ethan to her shoulder and patted his back. He quieted down. She glanced over at me and shrugged her shoulders. So much for his first swimming lesson.

"So, what's she going to do about the teaching position?" Darion asked me.

"I think she's going to turn it down," I said. "It doesn't pay squat and it's not worth missing Ethan's first year. We'll just tough it out."

Darion crunched into a carrot. "That's a good plan. It's time you can't get back."

"Says the workaholic."

"Part of the job," Darion said. He nudged Chance's boot. "At least I'm not hungover after being out half the night."

"Somebody's got to make the sacrifice," Chance grumbled from under his hat.

The girls headed our way. Jenny stood out with her crazy pink ponytails. Tina was so tiny that you couldn't even imagine the chubby baby she was holding had actually ever been housed inside her.

Corabelle's black hair whipped in the wind, like a goddess. Some things had changed about her over the years, but not that classic beauty. Even though I'd known her since I was in diapers myself, looking at her never failed to catch my full attention.

"You're up," Jenny said, dumping the wriggling toddler onto Chance's belly. She immediately rolled off and took off for the waves again. "Better catch her."

Chance shifted the hat, saw Phoenix making a beeline for the ocean, and jumped to his feet, mumbling something that sounded pretty colorful.

Jenny smacked him as he passed. "Don't teach her advanced cursing just yet," she said. "You know we can only get away with *damn* and *hell*."

I took Ethan from Corabelle. "Didn't much care for the Pacific?"

"It's like he knows," she said.

"I remember that day," Jenny said. She shuddered. "Don't ever get in that water again," she told Corabelle. "I so do not want to be fishing anybody else out."

Corabelle watched Chance chase Phoenix across the sand and said, "Everything important has happened on the beach. This is where you got yourself pregnant, if memory serves."

Jenny plopped down on a towel. "Point taken."

"I do believe somebody's first encounter with somebody was also here," she said to Tina.

"Gross, I have that in common with Jenny?" Tina said.

Darion choked on his carrot.

"Somebody do a Heimlich!" Jenny called.

Darion held up his hand. "I'm good," he said. "I didn't realize how much you all shared."

"Oh, we know all the good stuff," Jenny said. "We know all about getting busy under Tina's big skirt." She turned to Corabelle. "Are you the only friend who hasn't banged on this beach?"

I grabbed Corabelle's hand and pulled her down. Ethan immediately reached for her, and she took him back. "That can be arranged," I said.

Jenny tossed a potato chip at my head. "Gross. There are children present."

"Says the girl who conceived hers by a rock." I tossed the chip back.

Chance returned with Phoenix. "Maybe she should have a snack," he said. "Keep her in one place for thirty seconds."

Jenny pulled an applesauce pouch from her bag and handed it over. "Okay, I think we can all agree that this piece of oceanfront property has definite history for all of us."

Corabelle bounced Ethan on her knees. Her boobs jiggled in her bikini top, and I began to wonder how long we had to stay before I could get her home.

"I can't imagine living anywhere else," Tina said. "Even though I was late getting here."

"We always wanted to go to the school by the sea," Corabelle said to me. "And now we're pretty much done. You'll graduate before the end of the year."

"You can't leave!" Jenny said. "Our kids have to grow up together!" She passed another snack to Chance to keep Phoenix from toddling off again.

"We're not planning to go anywhere just yet," I said, pulling Corabelle and Ethan closer to me. The baby rested his chin on

Corabelle's shoulder and looked at me with big solemn eyes. He looked like Manuelito in that moment, and it struck me for the first time that the two boys of mine had so much in common. They had met only twice, but Rosa was bringing Manuel for two weeks at Thanksgiving. That wasn't too far away.

"Good," Jenny said. "Because I need my village."

Phoenix dropped her cup in the sand and pointed a stubby finger at the sky. "Buff-fly," she said.

"What's that, sweetie pie?" Jenny asked.

"Buff-fly," she said again.

Everyone looked up. At first, it seemed like it was about to snow, the way dark bits floated across the sky. But that was ridiculous. This was Southern California. Then I realized we were seeing the fluttering of wings.

Darion stood up. "It's the monarch migration," he said. "I've seen it once before, when I was a kid."

We all got to our feet. Even Phoenix was silent as the cloud of orange and black butterflies arrived, swooping, sailing, and flitting silently by.

Corabelle found my hand and squeezed it. I looked at her, staring up in awe at the thousands of winged creatures passing through our little beach party.

Tina stood the farthest forward and stretched out her hand. After a moment, a single butterfly paused for a second on one of her fingers, then fluttered off again.

She started crying, and Darion put his arm around her. Corabelle let go of me and stepped forward, Ethan on her shoulder. She held up her hand as Tina had. It took a minute, but a butterfly landed on her as well.

She turned to me, tears in her eyes. "Look at all of them," she said. "There are so many."

Jenny snapped pictures like crazy. The butterfly didn't leave Corabelle as the other had, just sat there, its wings fanning open and closed, lazily, as if it had nowhere else to be.

When Ethan was born, we recreated the butterfly mobile we had once made for Finn. Above his crib, the glitter-sprayed cutouts swayed whenever we brushed against them.

Now the sky was filled with the real thing, colorful, flitting by. Several took a break on our cooler and chairs, and Phoenix toddled over to them, fascinated.

Ethan waved his hands and the butterfly on Corabelle's finger fluttered higher, hovered over them, then settled on Ethan's fuzzy head.

"Oh!" Corabelle cried. "Look!"

I came up behind her. Ethan's eyes were wide, looking around at all the grown-ups staring at him.

"It doesn't want to leave you," Tina said quietly.

Ethan brushed his forehead with his arm, and this time the butterfly landed on my shoulder.

"See?" Tina said. "He belongs to you." She sat down and jerked a drawing pad from her bag. Her fingers flew as she sketched on an empty page.

"You should move along," I told the butterfly. The numbers were already thinning, the majority of them already past. "Your friends will worry about you."

It sat a moment more, wings slowly flapping, its antennae quivering, bright against my white T-shirt.

Then it took off, fluttering into the sky, until it mixed in with the others and we no longer knew which one it was.

"That was beautiful," Corabelle said. Tears were slipping down her cheeks.

"We were at the right place at the right time," I said.

"Again," she said.

I knew she was thinking of that astronomy class where we found each other after four years apart. If anything had gone differently — if I hadn't enrolled, if she hadn't moved here after getting kicked out of her first college — this moment would never have come.

But we had taken that class. And Jenny had hooked up with Chance. And Tina had decided to keep the doctor after insisting she never would go on a second date.

Because of all this, we were together now. And the moments that we thought were fleeting, like the passing of these butterflies, had come together to make something that would last forever.

THE END

FOREVER

There ain't nothing you can say
To make me turn away
There ain't nothing you can do
To make me take my love away from you
Because I said forever
And that's just what I'm gonna to do

There ain't nowhere you can go
That I won't get my walking shoes and follow
There ain't nowhere you can hide
That I won't find you with the love inside me
Because I said forever
And that's just what I'm gonna to do

How could you believe that I
Would ever have the need to say goodbye
All those years ago
I said the words that should have let you know
Because I said forever
And that's just what I'm gonna do

There ain't nothing you can say
There ain't nothing you can do
There ain't nowhere you can go
And there ain't nowhere you can hide

The FOREVER song is a real song! Hear it at
www.bradwhittington.com/forever.

Lyrics throughout this novel by Deanna's author friend,
singer-songwriter Brad Whittington.

Also by Deanna Roy

Don't miss the other books in the Forever Series

Stella & Dane: Stella is ready to blow out of her honky tonk town when a hot stranger rolls in on a Harley, leading to a dangerous romance that upsets the locals and sparks a tragedy that will change everyone's lives. (Romance)

Baby Dust. Abandoned by friends and haunted by what they've lost, five women forge friendships to survive the death of their babies. (Women's Fiction)

About Deanna Roy

Deanna is a passionate advocate for women who have lost babies. She founded the web site www.pregnancyloss.info in 1998 after the loss of her first baby and continues to run both online and in-person support groups for women who have endured this impossible loss. Find her on Facebook, Twitter, Instagram, Google+, and Goodreads.

Learn more about the author at
www.deannaroy.com

Your review on Amazon is appreciated—it makes a huge difference to authors when readers provide their reactions to a work.

Dedications by Forever Fans

♥ Patti C. ~ May she always know what a hero she is, in my eyes, and in the eyes of my children. Love, AK ♥

♥ Kristin H. ~ For my family by blood and my family by choice, I love you all! ♥

♥ Bianca M. ~ For my Husband, daughter, and son my Forever Family, I'll Love you Always ♥

♥ Tanya ~ To Jarred, father to our Forever Family. ♥

♥ Abbie Ball ~ For my family by blood and by choice I be with you no matter what. ♥

♥ Keri Greear ~ To the two most important men in my life. My dad(you were taken way too soon) and my hubs. <3 ♥

♥ Angela D ~ For the love of my life Jeremy, thank you for making me feel that I'm the most beautiful girl in the world. Also for showing me that true love really does last Forever! ♥

♥ Tinker17 ~ To the man of my dreams, Michael, I love you more than life. 41 years is not enough time. ♥

♥ Charity Chimni ~ Grandma and Grandpa forever loved and never forgotten! ♥

♥ Vanessa ~ You will always be loved and missed my angel. ♥

♥ Kat S. ~ For my Forever Family! Always there for each other no matter what! LLCforever! ♥

♥ Missy ~ For To Aaron, Emma, Ethan & Wyatt, my forever family who own my heart & soul ♥

♥ Letty Hernandez ~ Thank you hubs for watching the kids while I read. I love you Jesus! ♥

♥ Christi L. ~ To my wonderful husband, Ronnie. You will always be my Forever Love. ♥

♥ Sandy W. ~ To my husband Larry for all the happiness you have given me and the love you have for are family ♥

♥ Dot Jordaan ~ Tnx to my husband Piet for 45 years of marriage. You are my rock. Love you. ♥

♥ Mike Urbat ~ I dedicate this to my daughter Diana, my second chance. ♥

♥ Leona Bowman ~ To my best friend I had for over 30 yrs. I will love & miss you forever. ♥

♥ Amber Isenhour ~ Even with all the ups and downs life has thrown us, I am so lucky that I get to be a part of our Forever Family and I wouldn't change it for anything in the world!! ♥

♥ Ashley Spears ~ Marsha Pace, thank you for being the best sister, best friend, and best Auntie to my Angels and I. You have been my rock. Harold C., thank you for being there for me and caring about my girls more than their biological "father" ever has. You have been my rock as well more then you will ever know! I love y'all with all of my heart! ♥

♥ Marianne ~ To my mom, Ruth, for being my forever family ♥

♥ Chrissie ~ For Harvey - Fate decided our family wasn't meant to be beyond just the two of us. You are and always will be my Forever. ♥

♥ Tabby ~ Queen of Hearts with so much love to give. Love to all ♥

♥ Wendy R. ~ To my family and my close friends-thank you and love you! ♥

♥ Kim J. ~ For my Forever Family, Rob, Nick, and Maddie. You are my heart and soul. ♥

♥ Shirley ~ to my amazingly wonderful husband, Andy Thornton I love you with all my heart, body, and soul!!! You and our family are my whole world. ♥

♥ Kay Bennett ~ My husband Bill will not be on earth with me long...he is my friend and love always in my heart my family all mean the world to me. BILL will be with me forever in my heart....his days are numbered but BILL lives with me. ♥

♥ Lori S. ~ To the 5 best things in my life: Chris, Kayl, Nicholas, Emily & Erik ♥

♥ Jane ~ To my Forever Family, my husband, children and my three grandchildren. I love you so much!! ♥

♥ Jennifer Phillips ~ To the baby I lost in 2005, you'll always be part of my Forever Family. ♥

♥ Rochelle J. ~ For my wonderful husband, Jim, daughter Julie and my two wonderful grandsons! You are my Forever Family and I love you! ♥

♥ Jackie ~ To my husband and best friend, Ted Stieghorst. Love Always ♥

♥ Kristina L. ~ To Vic my best friend and my Prince Charming, I'll love you forever & always, you're my other half ♥

♥ Darla S. ~ For my love John, You truly are my soulmate. Luv You Muchly XOXO ♥

♥ Michelle Q. ~ To my brothers Chris and Lee, love you lots! ♥

♥ Angelina D. ~ To Matt and my kids. I love you all with everything I am. You all are my forever family ♥

♥ Katie Winter ~ Parker & Ridley Papcke ♥

♥ Melissa R. ~ To my wonderful grandson, Liam. You are my life and my light. Love you always, Grandma ♥

♥ Carrie Franks Fink ~ Our Family, no matter what the tragedy, we stand together. -Franks Family ♥

♥ Kari J. ~ To the One who stood beside me always! Love you 4 ever, DJ! ♥

♥ Debbie ~ To my angel StacyLynn love and miss you always. ♥

♥ Debbie Rice ~ My parents Buddy and Dotty Adams and my brother Lewie Adams you are forever in our hearts ♥

♥ J. Kogel ~ Here's to light at the end of the tunnel. ♥

♥ Melissa R. ~ To my husband, my best friend, my love. You and the kids are my life! ♥

♥ Lesley ~ To my sons Nathan and Jayson, we are Forever Family!! With all my Love, Mom!! ♥

♥ Lyndsi ~ I love you Matthew & Xander! I love you Cody! ♥

♥ Heather Brown ~ with much love to all my family ♥

♥ Sara Gómez ~ To the boy who made my heart feels and breaks, who made me brave and weak, who learnt me to love and hate. ♥

♥ Cassandra D: ~ For my one & only love, Stephen D, and the dreams we have to someday have our own Forever Family! I love you! ♥

Zeinab ~ I would like to dedicate this book to all those who were an inspiration and worked very hard to creat this amazing work and to the dearest man who has always owned my heart my mind my soul I love you my darling M. ♥

Kelly Richgruber ~ To the 3 most wonderful children i live you with all of my heart ♥

Cilicia White ~ To my wonderful husband Corbitt and my two beautiful kids Corbitt and Corrine! Love You Always ♥

Becky R. ~ For my true love Charles, thank you for being my partner in our Forever Family. ♥

Chasity Simmons ~ I dedication is to my mother who has supported me through some really rough times, I Love You ♥

Kamie E. ~ My beautiful daughter, Julie, who almost never made it into this world but survived all the odds! You are truly loved by everyone!! ♥

Cynthia Phillips ~ To my husband and our four amazing boys (Corbin, Dresdin, Emmit, Brody) I love you forever and always! ♥

Jodi ~ To my husband Joe who has always been there for me and to my Boys I Love You All you're My Forever Family! ♥

Debbie ~ To my beautiful son Thomas. I will always love you. Love Mom. ♥

Faith H. ~ To my mom, Katy for always being the wind beneath my wings ♥

Norma G. ~ For my forever family, my husband Cesar, my two miracles Luna and Christian, and my two little angels. Love you always. ♥

Katy Rakel ~ To my beautiful daughter who is my best friend, sister, and the most loving, faithful person I have ever known. I love you, Faith Hatch, bunches and bunches. You are the wind beneath my wings. Love, your mama ♥

LaGina ~ To Dawn, Virginia, Bobby and Cliffy, as much as I love my art I will never create anything more beautiful then the 4 of you. ♥

Cristal Nash ~ For my love Donald, if not for you we'd not have our own Forever Family ♥

- ♥ Karen Petrie ~ To the love of my life and my forever family...Mark, here is to 35 more years to come! ♥

- ♥ Nicole S. ~ To my monkey, I love you so much; Near or far. Love, Auntie. ♥

- ♥ G. Dixon ~ To my mother that would have been 85 years old today, I miss every day and wish you were here. You were my teacher,protector,but most of all my best friend. I love you. ♥

- ♥ Tater ~ Cooter, you are the love of my life and I could never have made it the last 13 years without you! ♥

- ♥ Erica ~ Best family ever, Ryan, Kyara, Rylee, Kayla. Love you all very much ♥

- ♥ Donna Hokanson ~ This dedication is to Dallas H., my best friend from my A.F. Family and whose life has been cut too short. May he be at peace. ♥

- ♥ Mom/Nana & Dad/Grandad ~ Our daughter, grandson (born @ 27 weeks), and grandaughter (stillborn @ 30 weeks). ♥

- ♥ Linda M. ~ For my husband Jerry.My love my blessing and my Forever Family. ♥

- ♥ Mike Urbat ~ To my daughter Diana who gave me a second chance ♥

- ♥ Kazza ~ To my husband John of 39 years of my forever family ♥

- ♥ Annie ~ For my amazing husband, Mathew, who has been my rock through each of my 11 miscarriages. I love you to the moon! ♥

- ♥ Irish Red ~ Boo, I love you & thank you for EVERYTHING you do for our Forever Family. You're the best! Love you so much! ♥

- ♥ Jessica H. ~ C,K,C I love you Always and 4ever ♥

- ♥ Brenda Prinsen ~ Matt, Scott, Heather, Nick, Nicole and Hailee you are my world, I love you. ♥

- ♥ Shandra Torbett ~ For Sarah Dockery, who has created the best Forever Family with me. ♥

- ♥ Cheri H. ~ To my Awesome Granddaughter, Morgan, who has felt the loss twice and has persevered. Your son and daughter await us in Heaven. God Bless! ♥

- ♥ JMM ~ JGM BMHTMS ♥

♥ Megan B. ~ For my little fighter Presley keep fighting we want you at home. You complete our family. ♥

♥ Sheri Weber ~ To my beautiful, amazing daughter Kaitlyn. You are the best thing that's ever happened to me and I'm proud to be your mama. I love you! ♥

www.ingramcontent.com/pod-product-compliance
Lightning Source LLC
Chambersburg PA
CBHW022030260626
47156CB00017B/1143